The Poison *That* Fascinates

Also by Jennifer Clement

Widow Basquiat
A True Story Based On Lies

The Poison *That* Fascinates

Jennifer Clement

CANONGATE
Edinburgh · London · New York · Melbourne

Jennifer Clement acknowledges the financial support of Mexico's Sistema
Nacional de Creadadores de Arte.

First published in Great Britain in 2008 by
Canongate Books Ltd, 14 High Street,
Edinburgh EH1 1TE

1

British Library Cataloguing-in-Publication Data
A catalogue record for this book is available on
request from the British Library

ISBN 978 1 84195 979 5

Typeset in Hoefler Text by Palimpsest Book Production Limited,
Grangemouth, Stirlingshire

Printed and bound by Mackays of Chatham plc, Chatham, Kent

www.canongate.net

CONTENTS

Female criminals are shorter than normal women; and in proportion to their stature, prostitutes and female murderers weigh more than honest women

Prostitutes have bigger calves than honest women

Female thieves and above all prostitutes are inferior to honest women in cranial capacity and cranial circumference

Criminals have darker hair than normal women, and this also holds good to a certain extent for prostitutes. Several studies of prostitutes, however, have found that in these women rates of fair and red hair equal and sometimes exceed those of normal women

Grey hair, which is rare in the normal woman, is more than twice as frequent in the criminal woman. On the other hand, in both young and mature criminal woman, baldness is less common than in normal women. Wrinkles are markedly more frequent in criminals of ripe years.

La Donna Delinquente (1893)
Cesare Lombroso and Guglielmo Ferrero

I.

A List of Pages

Page 4 can be very quiet.

Page 13 can be a torn dress.

Page 34 can be the month of April in Mexico.

Page 76 can be the scent of melons.

Page 83 can be a sanctuary.

Page 100 can be latitude 30 degrees south.

Page 108 can be a child lost in the forest.

Page 123 can be a child found in the forest.

Page 124 can be a child found in the forest who is not cold or hungry.

Page 185 can be a knife.

Emily Neale was raised on encyclopaedias and dictionaries. She likes to collect facts. She knows she can travel in an atlas and fall in love in a novel.

She knows she can kill someone in a book.

2.

She Likes to Collect Facts, Especially on Women Criminals

Emily knows about the saints of pencils, amputees, alpinists, circus people and clairvoyance. She knows that Saint Odilia heals the blind and that David is the patron saint of doves.

In Mexico saints are remembered every day.

There are saints for shipwrecks and broken bones.

There are saints for lost belongings.

There are saints for girls who forget to say their prayers at night.

Every morning on many of Mexico's radio and television stations the saints' days are announced along with the weather forecast and traffic report.

There are saints for misfortune, the ill fated, for those who are unlucky.

Mother Agata taught Emily about saints because she believes that saints can only help intercede or mediate if one knows about them. Every day is a celebration. On 19 April Mother Agata celebrates the saint for emergencies and on 23 August she honours the feast day for embroiderers. She claims that the primary reason she became a nun was to learn about saints and teach their lives to others.

Mother Agata is an enormous woman. Her hands are so large that she can carry most things in one hand. Dressed in her nun's habit she looks like a colossal angel that people stand beside for shade or shelter. Children want to climb up the trunk, limb and branch of her body. She smells like pith and bark. She smells like avocados.

Everyone who knows her thinks that she became a nun because no man could have loved such a large woman. No man could have withstood the humiliation of having to build a huge bed or gigantic chairs.

Emily thinks a man could get lost in her arms.

When Mother Agata goes to the market she does not take a shopping bag. She carries six eggs in her right hand and five tomatoes in her left.

Mother Agata lives at the Rosa of Lima Orphanage in Mexico City. Emily's great-grandmother founded the orphanage at the beginning of the twentieth century and recruited nuns, teachers and caretakers to help her. At first the orphanage was established for the children of mining families but, over the decades, accepted orphans from all kinds of backgrounds.

Emily works at the orphanage several days a week. This

is a family tradition. Her great-grandmother, her grand-mother and her mother worked there. Emily does not remember her mother, but her father tells her that it was her mother who hired Mother Agata to run the orphanage.

'Your mother came home one day,' Emily's father says, 'and reported she'd found the perfect person. She'd been interviewing for weeks trying to find someone appropriate. When your mother met Mother Agata she said she'd found a woman who was a doorway, could be a mother, and who understood that one cannot heal oneself by wounding another.'

Thanks to Mother Agata, Emily knows that this is a direct quote from Saint Ambrose. He is the patron saint of bees.

Mother Agata says that she is the kind of woman who sees swans when she looks at geese. 'I also like anything that is broken. All my children are broken,' she says. 'All my teacups are broken. I don't fix anything.' Emily thinks that Mother Agata is like a living oracle. She says things like 'You can rub words together to make a fire' and 'Words are not just the clothes of things.'

Emily's father calls Mother Agata 'The Giant'. He means it kindly because he is very fond of her. Everyone is. The children at the orphanage are terrified of her at first. They soon learn that she is a tree, a wall, and a church that casts shade.

Emily was born on 22 May, Saint Rita's feast day. The saint evoked against bleeding and desperate situations.

Raised alone by her father, a quiet, reserved man, Emily

had been the kind of child who could sit alone in the small garden for hours looking for insects or creating rivers with the garden hose. She walked around the house speaking quietly to herself and spent whole afternoons organising the drawers in the kitchen or drawing her own comic books. Like most solitary children, she could read the same book over and over again. Even as a child, her favourite books were encyclopaedias and almanacs, since she liked to read about people's lives and amazing facts. She and her father used to compete to see who could come up with the most amazing statistic or story. One of Emily's favourite books was the *Guinness Book of World Records*.

Emily attends the National Autonomous University of Mexico and works at the orphanage several times a week. At the university she studies history and is doing her thesis on the lives of saints. She also continues to exercise her childhood passion for strange information and likes to memorise facts on many subjects.

Emily has read that, in 1486, 20,000 people were sacrificed in Mexico during a single ceremony in dedication to the great Teocalli temple. She knows about scientific discoveries. She knows that salt is a compound made of sodium and chloride.

She knows these things:

The youngest survivor of the *Titanic* was Millvina Dean, who was eight weeks old at the time.

The parts of a pair of scissors are called handle, edge, pivot, blade and shank.

Andreas Vesalius discovered that men and women have the same number of ribs. One person in seventy has an extra rib and this occurs three times more commonly in males.

In 1816, a tooth belonging to Sir Isaac Newton was sold for over two thousand pounds. The English nobleman who bought it had it set into a ring.

A stethoscope conveys sounds from inside the body. There are two sounds in every heartbeat.

The hairiest woman, Julia Pastrana, was born in 1834 to an Indian tribe in Mexico. She was completely covered with hair except for her eyes. She was exhibited around the world in the 1850s and mummified on her death in 1860. She was still being exhibited in Norway and Denmark in the 1970s.

Sound is measured by decibels. 0 decibel is the faintest sound heard. 10-20 decibels is the sound of rustling leaves. 20-30 decibels is a whisper.

Her blood type is A Rh positive.

Emily collects facts the way some people collect stamps, coins or stones. She also likes to read about mysteries, detective stories and assassins, especially female assassins, and has two notebooks filled with facts on women criminals that she keeps in her bookcase in her bedroom. Emily knows that most women who kill are 'black widows' or 'medical murderers'. They kill for money, revenge, or commit 'mercy' or 'hero' killings. They are mostly gentle killers who prefer poison rather than risk physical confrontation.

Mother Agata thinks that Emily's interest in assassins is morbid.

'You've always loved weird tales. I wonder why,' Mother Agata asks her one day when Emily is sitting in the kitchen at the orphanage drinking coffee. 'And now I'm as interested in all of this as you are!'

'I just want to understand,' Emily answers. 'It's interesting to me – they're stories, histories. In any case, I'm trying to find out if at heart I am a forensic scientist, a detective or a criminal . . .' she adds, laughing.

Emily knows, from the many books that she has read, that the weapons of women are in teacups, sinks, cabinets and thimbles – places where poisons can be hidden. She also knows that a word can be a knife. A tear can be a sword.

'You'll never understand because you were raised not to understand. In any case, no civilised person can understand murder,' Mother Agata answers and pours herself another cup of coffee.

'Do you understand?' Emily asks.

'I understand and know that a person can do anything. Betrayal is easy and, under certain circumstances, killing is as easy too. I sometimes think that history is the memory of murder.'

Mother Agata reads the newspaper from cover to cover every morning. She takes a pair of scissors out of a glass jar on her desk and cuts out the murder stories or stories having to do with interesting facts and gives them to Emily. She has done this for years. Emily keeps the stack of these clippings inside a drawer in the dressing table at home in her bedroom. Many have grown yellow and brittle over time.

Mother Agata sighs and hands Emily a perfectly cropped newspaper clipping. 'I think you'll like this one. It was published in yesterday's newspaper and I saved it for you. Actually, I *know* you'll like this one. It is about a nun who killed another nun.'

'How interesting . . .'

'This is something very strange, don't you think? A woman killing another woman. I can't remember reading anything like this before. And to think she is a daughter of God!'

'Many women have killed women. It is not really that unusual. So, why did the nun do it? Does the newspaper give a reason?'

'Yes, the nun herself explains why. Go ahead and read it for yourself,' Mother Agata answers, cupping her hand over her mouth. 'It says right here in black and white that it was because the nun had had it. She was tired of being pinched and tickled all the time. A perfect reason, don't you think?'

Fact:

Crimes Punishable by the Death Penalty in the state of California, USA: first-degree murder with special circumstances; treason; perjury causing execution; train wrecking.

Louisa Peete, who was born Lofie Louise Preslar, changed her name to 'Anna Lee'. She wanted to have a glamorous, movie star name.

'Anna Lee' told fantastic stories. They were so incredible that everyone believed them. It was impossible to imagine that a person could invent such ridiculous stories.

She said one of her favourite lovers had disappeared because he quarrelled with a 'Spanish-looking woman' who chopped his arm off with a sword. Later she said that it had actually been his leg and that he was recuperating in some hidden location because he did not like to show weakness.

She said another lover disappeared because he believed he was the reincarnation of Sir Walter Raleigh and left to go live in London. 'Anna Lee' claimed that he liked to pretend that her house was a ship.

Clinton Duffy, San Quentin's warden, described 'Anna Lee' as bearing 'an air of innocent sweetness that masked a heart of ice'.

In her belongings the police found a peacock-blue silk purse that contained dozens of white buttons that she'd cut off the shirts of her victims.

3.

The Rosa of Lima Orphanage

It is on the day that 'The Japanese' arrive at the orphanage that Emily first notices abnormal things happening in her house. Some nights she thinks she hears the sound of a door opening and someone whispering or humming quietly.

She finds a banana peel in her wastebasket.

Emily also notices that some things are out of place: in the kitchen she finds spoons in the drawer for knives.

On the mornings that Emily does not go to university, she visits the orphanage. The Neale family founded the Rosa of Lima Orphanage in honour of Pedro Romero de Terreros, who was a miner and a philanthropist. He was born in 1710 in Cartagena, Spain, and died in Mexico. Emily's great-grandmother had been fascinated by the stories that were still told about this man and his great wealth. When she read that he had stipulated that a fifth of his profits from his sliver mines should go to the establishment of an orphanage, she decided that the Neale family would do the same.

The orphanage was established in a seventeenth-century colonial building near to the Neales' residence in Coyoacan. Originally, the orphanage had been a coffee warehouse. When the Neale family bought the house it had been abandoned for several years. As much as they washed and scrubbed, the scent of coffee never left the site.

The square-shaped structure was built with two storeys, which was unusual for that time, around an inner courtyard. The orphans sleep on the second floor and the office, classrooms, kitchen and Mother Agata's rooms are on the first floor. Emily's great-grandmother had a plaque of black iron made for the entrance to the building that says 'Home to Every Child. The Rosa of Lima Orphanage. 1905.'

Mother Agata says that she thinks this is the perfect name for an orphanage. 'This saint,' she explains, 'refused to marry and she rubbed her face with pepper so she'd look unattractive.'

In the centre of the orphanage's courtyard there is a small, round stone fountain covered in white and blue Talavera tiles. The water emerges from a spout under a very simple carved stone cross with a discreet motif of grape leaves carved into the stone. The walls surrounding the courtyard are painted dark blue. The doorways and windows are framed with bands of yellow paint.

Emily arrives at the orphanage at the moment when two new children, who are cousins, are being received. Their names are Maria and Hipolito. Maria is nine years old and

Hipolito is ten. They are oriental-looking so they have immediately been nicknamed 'The Japanese' by the other orphans. The children say that Maria looks just like the drawing of the woman on the package of Japanese peanuts.

Maria and Hipolito's parents were driving a pickup truck that was transporting corn from Puebla to Mexico City. The cousins were in the back of the pickup truck, sitting among the sheaves, when the truck was hit head-on by a politician driving a silver BMW at 140 kilometres an hour. Both sets of parents were killed. The children were thrown into the road and, although they were critically injured, both survived.

Maria and Hipolito arrive at the orphanage in an ambulance provided by the hospital. They look so strange that nobody speaks to them for a few minutes. Everyone stares. Some of the children cover their mouths. Mother Agata stands still with her great long arms falling down the sides of her body.

'The Japanese' look strange because their clothes are odd pieces of material: trousers with one leg only, a shirt without sleeves. Hipolito is wearing one shoe. A white sock covers his other foot. Maria's skirt is fixed to her waist with a rope and the right sleeve hangs loosely from the shoulder of her brown sweater. It takes everyone a few seconds to realise that their clothes have been cut in order to fit around white plaster casts.

Mother Agata becomes so agitated at the sight of these

two children that she suddenly begins to skip and jump without moving from the place where she stands. Her large hands reach out to the children in spastic motions but she does not touch. Nobody wants to touch them.

Emily thinks they could break.

Mother Agata immediately lights a candle to the saint of broken bones: Stanislaus Kostka.

Maria and Hipolito constantly kiss and burrow against each other. They cannot hug or hold hands because of their plaster casts. Emily thinks that it is as if they can only stand the pain that each other gives, the shared pain. They are all that is left of a life they once knew. They see their parents' faces in each other's eyes.

Hipolito remembers watching ants, making bonfires with burning rubber tyres at Christmas, and the bicycle his mother had promised to buy for him on his next birthday. Maria remembers custards and pineapple water. Their favourite word is: remember.

'The Japanese' whisper silently to each other. Mother Agata assigns them their beds and says that Maria will sleep in the 'girls' dormitory', which is on the left side of the building, and Hipolito will sleep in the 'boys' dormitory', which is on the right. 'The Japanese' suddenly look stricken. They declare emphatically that they want to sleep in the same bed. Mother Agata stares at them in silence, frowns and presses her lips together.

'That is absolutely fine with me,' Mother Agata says after

a few moments and touches the palms of her hands together as if in prayer. 'That will be no problem, no problem at all. Yes, yes, I understand completely.'

She asks one of the nuns who occasionally work at the orphanage to look at all the beds and decide which one is largest. She also explains that they will have their own room and says that she will clean out one of the pantries by the kitchen. 'Those pantries really smell like coffee, but you'll just have to get used to it. It can't be helped. The smell is in the very pores of this building.'

'The Japanese' nod. 'I like coffee,' Maria says.

'So do I,' Hipolito answers in a whisper as if he is afraid that any loud noise could make his body hurt even more.

'We'll get the carpenter to build a larger bed if need be,' Mother Agata continues as she places her hand on Hipolito's head as if she were blessing him.

Mother Agata announces that since the children's injuries do not allow them to play or attend the primary classes at the orphanage everyone must read to them until they get better. The other orphans agree as they circle 'The Japanese', examining their bodies and trying to figure out where the white plaster casts begin and end.

When Emily returns to her home, after being at the orphanage most of the day, she finds her father resting in the living room. He is listening to Agustin Lara on an old record player:

Woman, divine woman,
you have the poison that fascinates in your eyes,
woman you have the perfume
of an orange tree in bloom.

He puts down the newspaper and continues to sip on his glass of tequila. Emily kisses his cheek and sits down beside him.

He is her only family. He is her father, mother, brother and sister. He kept Emily close to him. At the same time he made sure that Emily was part of the orphanage, since it was a place she could also call home. She used to spend a lot of time there, even as a child, although she also attended an expensive British school.

Emily knows she is half an orphan. As a child she used to think of things that were halves of other things. She used to look up words in the dictionary: half-ripe, half-empty, a half note, half-moon, half-hearted, half-light, half-truth, half-and-half. She knows that this is what enabled the orphans to accept her over the years.

Emily's father met her mother in London in 1963 at a party held at the Mexican embassy. She was studying to be an architect and Emily's father had just finished his degree at the London School of Economics.

'When I asked her if she wanted to leave London and move to Mexico she didn't hesitate. She took to Mexico immediately,' Emily's father explained to her over the years.

'It was as if she had lived here her whole life. I've seen this happen to many people who come to this country. They can never leave or they spend the rest of their lives wanting to return.'

Emily's father never remarried. He spent the remainder of his life devoted to his daughter, his work at the bank and his position as honorary director of the orphanage. He also fills up his time by doing research on the disappearance of butterflies, moths and beetles from the Valley of Mexico. He has boxes filled with the specimens of his childhood: large yellow and white butterflies, brittle beetles and furry moths with large black spots on their wings. His most unusual specimens are kept folded in pieces of green felt.

Emily takes hold of her father's hand and tells him about the arrival of 'The Japanese' at the orphanage. She looks into his face. He has a high forehead and large blue eyes with specs of white in the iris. His skin is fair and dry and freckled from a lifetime of too much sun.

'These children are so sweet,' Emily says. 'They have already been nicknamed. The others are calling them "The Japanese", which you'll see is so perfect when you meet them. And they're cousins so they have a little bit of family left – each other. Mother Agata has let them sleep in their own room since they don't want to be separated.'

'How old are they?'

'I didn't ask. But they look about eight or nine. They seem so bewildered, which, as you know, is so often the case at the beginning. I think that they're both still in shock. Their broken bones have yet to heal.'

'What happened to the politician who crashed into their truck?' Emily's father asks. He reaches for the bottle of tequila and pours another short glass of the transparent liquid.

'Nobody knows. Or nobody says. Mother Agata says that it doesn't matter since nothing will bring those parents back.'

'She's right. Nevertheless,' he adds as he stands up, places his hands on his hips and arches his back in a long stretch, 'you can be sure that nothing happened to him. He's probably in Acapulco having a good time!'

'Yes, I'm sure you're right.'

Outside they hear the high-pitched whistle of the man who sharpens knives. Every three days he comes past the house on a bicycle rigged with a whetstone.

'Over the decades I've known so many children with so many strange stories,' Emily's father adds. 'Sometimes it's unbearable. To this day I'll never forget one little boy who never said a word. His name was Pedro and he was found living in a tree in Chapultepec Park. He ran around like a squirrel. He liked to hide things in his armpits, in his mouth and in his clothes. It even made the papers. He must have been about seven years old and he never learned to speak so we never really knew what had happened to him. In his early teens he ran away from the orphanage.'

Emily's father frowns and takes another sip from his glass

of tequila. He offers some to Emily, but she declines, shaking her head.

'I am too tired,' she says and yawns. 'I just want to go to bed. I have an exam tomorrow.'

'By the way,' her father asks as he lifts himself up from his armchair to kiss her cheek, 'were you in my room today?'

'No,' Emily answers. 'Why?'

'Oh, I was just wondering . . . someone left the window open.'

Emily goes up the stairs to her bedroom, which is at the far end of the house and above the front gate. In her room the counterpane on her bed has been turned down and her pillow has been taken off the bed and placed on the floor. It looks as if the pillow were placed there in order to kneel on and pray.

Emily leans over, picks up the pillow, dusts it off with her hand and puts it back on the bed. She looks around the room to see if anything else has been disturbed. She checks the lock on the window, but it has not been touched.

Emily thinks she can smell the faint, sweet scent of melons.

Fact:

'If'n you don't listen to me, woman, I ain't gonna be here next week.'
Frank Harrelson, 2nd husband's final words

'*It must have been the coffee.*'
Arlie Lanning, 3rd husband's last words

'*He had been making me mad, shining up to other women.*'
Nannie Doss, about 4th husband Richard Morton

Nannie Doss was born in Dixie in 1905. She loved to read 'True Romance' magazines. At her trial she explained that she was always living in search of a perfect man. 'That's about it,' she said. 'I was searching for the perfect mate, the real romance of life.'

    Her two children died.
    Her first husband died.
    Her third husband died.
    Her fourth husband died.
    Her sixth husband died.

    Six people.

She liked to dream about being carried across a threshold. She liked to dream about: bouquets of roses, boxes of chocolates, wedding rings, honeymoons, Ferris wheels and cotton candy.
    At her trial she explained that she was always living in search of a perfect man. 'That's about it,' she said. 'I was searching for the perfect mate, the real romance of life.'
    Arsenic is an element. It is found in opal glass, ceramics, enamels,

paints, wallpapers, weedkillers, insecticides, rodenticides, pesticides,
textile printing, tanning and taxidermy.

    'He wouldn't let me watch my favourite programmes on the tele-
vision,' she explained, 'and he made me sleep without the fan on the
hottest nights. He was a miser and, well, what's a woman to do
under those conditions?'

    Arsenic is a grey metal. Grey as grey clouds. Grey as grey pave-
ment.

    At her confession she said, 'If their ghosts are in this room they're
either drunk or sleeping.'

4.

Memories About Mexico City

In Mexico City there are only two seasons in a year: the rainy season and the dry season. During the dry season everything in the city seems to turn into stone – stone birds, stone flowers, stone butterflies. The sun warms the red pock-marked volcanic stone and the cement buildings and pavements burn. In the rainy season the city becomes molten, streets turn into rivers that carry plastics, newspaper, dry willow leaves and small shards of volcanic glass. The volcanoes and mountains that surround Mexico City are like the walls of a fortress that keep everyone out and keep everyone in.

One of Emily's father's favourite subjects is to discuss everything that has disappeared in Mexico City. Along with butterflies, moths and beetles, he has a long list of other related data. These fill him with anger, frustration and sadness.

The list includes trolley cars, pepper trees, garter snakes, rivers and lakes, bats, and the forests that once surrounded Mexico City.

As he and Emily sit together in the library he says that one of the worst things that has happened to the world is the discovery of electricity. This is because the night and all its creatures have disappeared. He complains about this as he examines a large hornworm moth with a broken wing.

In this list he includes things like the destruction of parklands and historical buildings.

Emily thinks that he does not mention her mother, who also disappeared from Mexico City like the trolley cars, pepper trees and rivers.

As Emily's father reads his books on beetles he listens to the music of Agustin Lara. The romantic songs '*Woman*', '*Love of My Loves*', '*Adventurer*', '*Night of the Ronda*' and '*Veracruz*' fill the house in Coyoacan with whimsical piano chords.

Emily knows all the lyrics since she has heard them over and over again since she was a child:

> *In the eternal night*
> *of my sadness*
> *you have been the star*
> *that lights the earth*
> *and I have divined*
> *your rare beauty*

and you have lit
my darkness.

And

Your black eyes like two fists,
your black eyes like two fists.

Emily's father remembers when Agustin Lara died in 1970.
At his funeral, thousands walked through the streets in
downtown Mexico City and a minute of silence was
observed in many places throughout the nation.

Mother Agata says that Emily's father exaggerates about
most things. She adds that there are also some bad things
that have disappeared, like polio. She remembers when some
of the children at the orphanage had polio and were forced
to wear metal leg braces and walk with crutches that were
permanently attached to their arms with metal cuffs.

'In the month of May, everyone avoided public swimming
pools, parks and crowded buses. The theatres were empty
and nobody went to visit the zoo,' Mother Agata explains.

One closet at the orphanage is still filled with half a dozen
metal leg braces, which stand like ancient armour in a
museum.

Mother Agata also adds that rats have disappeared.

'I remember when I used to kill two a day with a broom,'
she says. 'They were enormous with thick, dry tails. I don't

know if there is a saint for rats,' she adds, laughing. 'Maybe I need to look that up!'

Mother Agata also teaches the children about superstitions. 'I know it is a sin to be superstitious,' she says, 'but I'd rather confess to my superstitions than give them up. The priest says he understands. There are things that are born in us and cannot be helped. There's no proof, but I've seen them work even if I don't believe in a lot of them. We have to do anything we can against being unlucky. We're all unlucky and that's a fact. I remember a gardener – Jose Flores was his name. A perfect name for a gardener! Well, he was always walking under that ladder that he'd prop up against the wall so he could trim the ivy. I always told him not to do that. I told him he was asking for it and he just laughed at me. Well, I won't even tell anyone what happened to him! He ate a poisonous mushroom!'

Emily lives in the Coyoacan neighbourhood of Mexico City with her father. They inhabit the same summer/country house that Emily's great-grandfather built over one hundred years ago when he came to Mexico from Britain. The grounds that once had stables, a special room for baking bread and tortillas, as well as a large garden, are all gone since many decades ago they were sold off as land. Only the house and small interior garden remain.

The house is still filled with the things Emily's great-grandfather bought and shipped to Mexico. There is a large cedarwood linen chest, two oak armchairs, etchings of

British castles, two dressing tables with oval mirrors, dining room chairs, and a long oak dining room table. In the hallway a tall grandfather clock with half-moon pediments still chimes the time at every hour.

The library contains a large book collection that was boxed and sent to Mexico with the furnishings. It contains the collected works of Shakespeare, novels by the Brontë sisters, the collected works of Charles Dickens, a book of poems by Robert Burns, Homer's *Ulysses*, a leatherbound edition of the King James Bible, and a worn copy of Charles Darwin's *On the Origin of Species*. Among the books there are also encyclopaedias, almanacs, an atlas, cookbooks, dozens of seed catalogues, etiquette and hygiene books, and biographies on the lives of explorers like James Cook and David Livingstone.

In the garden roses grow from seeds that were brought over by her great-grandmother. There is dog-rose and sweetbrier. Every few years a periwinkle will appear under the kitchen window beside an ancient dark green cactus.

Emily's great-grandfather sent his children back to boarding schools in England, where they stayed and never returned. Only Emily's grandfather, with his British wife, returned to Mexico. Emily's father and his brother, her Uncle Charles, were also sent to boarding school at the age of seven. This was the custom practised by most British families in Mexico at that time.

Emily's great-grandfather came to Mexico to seek his

fortune in the silver mines. He leased a mining property outside the city of Pachuca, near Mexico City, where he quarried one small silver mine known as 'Silver Stone', which supported the family for decades.

In Emily's house they still have a few of the very first things fashioned from this initial silver vein. The first thing the family ordered made by the local silversmiths was a cross, followed by an ornate teapot and six silver spoons.

Emily's father only had one brother, Charles, who left Mexico City and went to live in Chihuahua, where he owned a farm and raised cattle. He was the only member of the Neale family who married a Mexican. Over the years, when Emily asked her father about this uncle, he always answered in a dismissive tone. 'He never really belonged,' her father said. 'He had wanderlust and always hated this city.' After Charles died Emily's father said that he was never able to locate his brother's widow and their only son, who was named Santiago.

When Emily asked Mother Agata about her Uncle Charles she'd say, 'He was a funny one. He was angry all the time, but he couldn't stand to see people suffer. People used to make fun of him because of this. Or, rather, other children made fun of him. He had a strange nature. He'd cry if he saw a street dog. I understood him. Of course he was a grown man when I met him, but you could always see the child there in him. Your father is so different. I think your

26

father has always been a grown-up. Your mother used to say he was an old shoe!'

Emily's father makes lists of things that have disappeared and tells Emily that someday he plans to publish them. 'I feel destruction around me,' he says. 'This is why I have tried to keep at least some of the past in this house. I have never replaced the old with the new.'

'Well,' Emily answers, 'I am so happy that you never threw away those old stacks of almanacs and turn-of-the-century periodicals since I love to read them and they do tell me about the past.'

Emily recalls the day that she found them in the library packed inside a window seat that opened into a small cupboard. The clever storage space had been forgotten so long ago that only a lonely child in a quiet house could have found it. Emily was ten years old when she noticed that the seat beneath her also had a hinge. When she opened it she found the periodicals bound in brown paper.

'They were probably saved to be used to light the fire-place,' her father had explained at the time. This seemed consistent since the secret cupboard also contained two small bundles of kindling wood tied together with string.

Emily read through these periodicals for years and knew some of them practically by heart. She specifically enjoyed reading the medical advertisements that included cures for baldness and infertility, and ways to make oneself taller. Her favourite was the advertisement for Dr Williams' Pink Pills, which promised to cure melancholy. The drawing in the periodical was disturbing. It showed a man slumped in an armchair with his head in his hands in a pose of defeat. The text stated the following: Melancholy. He who suffers from this sickness is worthy of compassion. To always be sad and dejected without animation, without ambition, but at the same time in good health is not an enviable condition.

'Those old periodicals are certainly a lesson in everything that has disappeared,' Emily's father says. 'It was quite a treasure you found . . .'

'It is a very dark evening,' Emily interrupts as she hears a scratching noise in the street. She stands up and walks over to the window and looks outside. A young woman walks past the house carrying a baby in her arms. 'There's nobody,' Emily says.

'It must have been the wind,' her father answers.

'Do you smell melons?' Emily asks.

'No. Do you?'

'Yes. I've smelt them for days. There must be a flower blooming . . .'

Fact:

Was it a blue dress? Was it a yellow dress? Was it a white dress?

It was a cheap cotton calico dress of light blue background with dark figures printed on it.

On Sunday morning, 2 August 1892, she burned her dress in the kitchen oven. The cotton threads burned and mixed with the ashes of bread and oats.

When Lizzie Borden was asked why she'd burned the dress she said it had paint on it.

Was it blue paint? Was it yellow paint? Was it white paint?

During the investigation Officer Mullaly asked Lizzie if there were any hatchets in the house. 'Yes,' she said. 'They are everywhere.'

In the basement there were four hatchets. Two were covered with dust. One had dried cow's blood and hair on it. One did not have a handle.

These were some questions and answers:

Q. *Where were you when your father came home?*

A. *I was down in the kitchen, reading an old magazine that had been left in the cupboard, an old* Harper's Magazine.

Q. *Where were you when the bell rang?*

A. *I think in my room upstairs.*

Q. *Then you were upstairs when your father came home?*

A. *I was on the stairs when she (Bridget) let him (Andrew) in . . . I had only been upstairs long enough to take the clothes up and baste the little loop on the sleeve. I don't think I had been up there over five minutes.*

Q. *. . . You remember that you told me several times that you were downstairs and not upstairs, when your father came home? You have forgotten, perhaps?*

A.   *I don't know what I have said. I have answered so many questions and I am so confused I don't know one thing from another. I am telling you just as nearly as I know.*

Q.   *. . . Which now is your recollection of the true statement of the matter, that you were downstairs when the bell rang and your father came in?*

A.   *I think I was downstairs in the kitchen.*

Q.   *And then you were not upstairs?*

A.   *I think I was not because I went up almost immediately, as soon as I went down, and then came down again and stayed down.*

5.

When Things Are Out of Place, and Emily Begins to Worry

Emily thinks of the word 'intruder'.

She thinks of the words 'trespasser' and 'prowler'.

One morning, two days after Emily finds the pillow removed from her bed and placed on the floor, she visits the orphanage. As she enters she finds that the children are gathered in the building's inner courtyard lined up to get on the school bus and go to the National Anthropology Museum. Since Emily is studying history at the university, Mother Agata asks her to come along as their guide.

'The Japanese' are unable to leave the orphanage because their injuries are still too grave for them to move around easily. Mother Agata sets them up at the kitchen table with a large jug of lemonade and a plate of toffee candies made from goat's milk. On the table she has also laid out large pieces of thick cardboard drawing paper and pots of paint and paintbrushes. She tells them to go ahead and paint whatever they like and that everyone will be back in a few hours. 'The Japanese' nod and stare at the empty pieces of white paper as if they were large mirrors.

In the courtyard Emily pins name tags on all the children and leads them on to the orange school bus outside the front door.

'Is everyone here?' Mother Agata asks. 'Has there been a head count?'

'All twenty-two of them,' Emily answers as she checks the names off on a piece of paper. 'Maria and Hipolito are staying, which would have made twenty-four. That's quite a large family you have.'

'Yes,' Mother Agata says. 'I think it's the most we've ever had. Certainly we can't take in any more.'

'Yes, it's really too many,' Emily agrees as they begin to move down the road. 'My father says that my great-grand-mother opened the orphanage with one child – the daughter of a Scottish miner who had lost both her parents to typhoid. Her name was Lizzie MacDonald. She was six years old – old enough to know what she had lost.'

'Yes, that's right. She was the first one. When she was eighteen she went back to Scotland and never returned to Mexico as far as I know. I think she thought she'd find her parents. Orphans always have these unbreakable ideas.'

'Someone ought to write a book that documents every-thing that happened to the orphans from the Rosa of Lima Orphanage. Perhaps I'll do it . . .' Emily says.

When they arrive at the museum Mother Agata first leads them outside to the Paseo de la Reforma Avenue to look at Tlaloc, the Rain God, which is a gigantic monolithic stone statue dating between 400 and 600 AD.

'Do you know,' Emily explains to the children, 'that when the statue was brought to Mexico City the electrical and telephone wires had to be raised or removed so the special vehicle that was carrying it could get through the city streets?'

The children look up and stare at the great stone face.

'It was brought into the city during the dry season but, as he entered, there was suddenly a massive thunderstorm with terrible flash flooding. Everyone knows this,' Mother Agata adds. 'At the time it was seen as some sort of an omen.'

As they walk through the enormous halls of the museum and look into the glass display cases, the children are fascinated by the small, fragile clay figures that represent duality: feminine figures with two heads or two faces.

Emily leans close to Mother Agata. 'They seem so taken with those odd figures. Have you noticed?'

'Orphans are always looking for mothers,' Mother Agata says to Emily with a deep sigh. Emily knows this is the reason Mother Agata always gives the children dolls and baby bottles as birthday or Christmas presents. 'Orphans are always looking for mothers,' she says again. 'It is terrible when you think that most children lose their mothers because the fathers kill them. At least the statistics are very alarming. Over the years many, many of our children lost their mothers this way.'

As they stroll through the museum Emily explains human sacrifice to the children. She tells them the myth of the Fifth Sun. This myth states that the sun needs to be fed with divine food – the blood and hearts of enemies captured in combat – so that humanity will not perish.

'Throughout history, sacrifice has appeared in many different forms,' she explains.

The children look at her attentively, taking in every word. They are so quiet that Emily thinks they must be listening to the beat of their own hearts.

When they finish their stroll through the museum, Mother Agata and Emily sit together on a bench while the orphans run around the open courtyard's large, interior fountain. The boldest children get close to the stream of water and scream out loud when they get wet.

Emily notices that one of the children is wearing a bright red cardigan with a green Christmas tree on it. 'Is that mine?' Emily asks. 'I seem to recall having something exactly like it . . .'

'Of course,' Mother Agata answers. 'That is your cardigan. It's a hand-me-down. Perhaps you weren't aware of this, but all your old clothes were always sent to the orphanage. The children have been wearing your clothes for years.'

'That's funny. I never noticed it before. It's strange to

think of someone wearing your clothes. It's like they've taken on your armour or become you somehow.'

'Don't be ridiculous,' Mother Agata says.

'But I remember feeling so powerful when I wore that sweater. Honestly, I remember this perfectly.'

'They're only clothes.'

'Yes, of course,' Emily repeats. 'They're only clothes. You wear God's clothes, as a nun, I mean . . .'

'Yes, I suppose you're right.'

As they continue to watch the children play Emily turns toward Mother Agata. 'What was I like as a child?' she asks.

'You were kind and sweet and good,' Mother Agata answers circling Emily with her arm. 'You slept with your fists clenched tight as if you were waiting for a fight. In the morning your poor hands would ache so badly that I had to rub them for you.'

'I still do it,' Emily answers.

'And then there was always the little chirp of a bird around the house. It was just you talking to yourself. You'd ring the doorbell, open the door and pretend that visitors had arrived to see you. You'd serve them tea or show them around. You were always making up your own games. Can a child be too obedient, too good? I think orphans are often too sweet and passive. This is because they are so afraid of losing more people in their lives.'

Emily moves away from Mother Agata and stands up so that she can look at Mother Agata face-on. She can hear the cries of the children running behind her mixed with the forceful sound of water falling from the fountain.

'Actually,' Emily says, 'this is no game this time. I need to talk to you about something important.'

'What is it?' Mother Agata replies, turning her gaze away from the children and looking deeply into Emily's face. 'Speak up.'

'The first thing that happened is that my bed covers were opened and my pillow lay on the floor. Then I found two of my books on the floor. Another evening one of my dresses had been taken out of the closet and placed on my bed. The sleeves were spread out and the back zipper had been pulled down.'

'Did you speak to Laura, the servant?' Mother Agata asks.

'Yes,' Emily answers. 'Of course. That was the first thing I did. She says she knows nothing about it. And of course it wasn't her. It makes no sense.'

'No, of course it wasn't her,' Mother Agata repeats. 'It is very strange. Maybe you should come and stay at the orphanage for a while. This is frightening.'

'Nothing has actually been taken. Things are just moved around, out of place.'

Mother Agata sits quietly for a moment. Her fists are deep inside the large pockets a seamstress makes for her large hands.

'I feel as if someone is coming into my room while I am away from home. I've checked the windows and locks but everything looks untouched.'

'Have you told your father?' Mother Agata asks.

'I haven't wanted to alarm him,' Emily answers. 'You know how upset he can get over the smallest things. Also, to be honest, it's taken me a little time to sort of take it in. I didn't give it much importance at first. I thought I was just being absent-minded. But I am beginning to feel that something needs to be done. Maybe we need to hire someone to watch the house.'

'Promise to let me know if anything else happens.'

'I'm going to wait a few days before telling my father. I thought I should let you know so that someone outside of the house knows about this.'

When they get back to the orphanage they find that 'The Japanese' are still sitting in the kitchen. They have painted dozens of pickup trucks in red, blue and yellow paint. Some of the vehicles have drawings of corn stalks in them. One red pickup truck is drawn with two small children, painted as stick figures, falling out of the vehicle while a colossal blue car drives toward it. Everybody looks at the drawings in silence.

'We were trying to remember what our pickup truck looked like,' Maria says. Hipolito nods his head in agreement.

'I remember it was red,' Maria says.

'I remember it was blue,' Hipolito says.

'It was full of corn. We were taking the corn to the market,' Maria says.

'Yes,' Hipolito echoes, 'it was full of corn. We were taking the corn to the market.'

'It must be true,' Maria adds. 'It must be true since we both remember.'

'It doesn't matter,' Mother Agata answers in a soft, soothing voice. 'These are beautiful drawings. We'll hang them up in the reading room so that everyone can look at them.'

When Emily gets home from the orphanage and walks up the stairs to her room, she finds the drawers in her dresser pulled open. Nothing has been taken.

Fact:

A very expensive love potion:
A glass of red wine
2 sticks of cinnamon
2 apples
10 raisins
The body of a child

Marti Enriqueta knew what brews to make for every situation. She had teas for unfaithful wives, drinks for lost loves and perfumes for people suffering from hysteria. Millán Astray, head of the police department, said, 'She was that kind of ancient witch who would have been burned at Zocodover.'

Marti Enriqueta was well known for curing melancholy. Her

prescription for this was to have the patient walk across the deck of an old ship. She said that melancholy was the very worst of illnesses since it made people turn yellow, from the thickening of the blood, and was a spiritual condition – the collapse of body and soul.

For menstruating women she advised softly beating their stomachs with a spoon. If someone was suffering from uncontrollable spasms they were advised to say the word 'stop' a hundred times a day for three months.

Marti Enriqueta was arrested in Barcelona, Spain, in 1912 for kidnapping and killing several children. She had made her living by selling her charms and potions. These were written in a book bound with human hair.

An inexpensive love potion:
A glass of water
2 apples
10 teardrops.

6.

A Famous Story About a Brother and a Sister

In Emily's father's list of things that have disappeared in Mexico City he includes telegrams. He remembers the young boys who arrived at the house on bicycles to deliver them throughout the day. He recalls the brown, undersized envelope and reading the stark staccato language.

When a telegram arrives at the house he is so astonished that he greets Emily at the front door as soon as she gets home. He reads it aloud to her as they walk together down the hallway toward the library. 'Arrival. Thursday. Will call. Nephew. Santiago.' Emily's father says 'stop' between each word. 'Em, I don't think a telegram has come to this house in twenty-five years at least. There are people, like you in fact, who have never received a telegram in their lifetime.'

'What do you think it means? Do you think he plans to stay here? It's not very clear is it?'

'No, you'd think he would have telephoned. I have to say

I like the fact that he sent a telegram. It reminds me of the telegrams we used to get from London.'

'Maybe he only had the address, and God knows the postal service is so poor . . .'

'Well, we'll see what he's like. Is there anything we need to do? Do we need to prepare anything?' Emily's father asks. 'I wonder what he'll look like . . .'

The following day at the orphanage Emily tells Mother Agata about the telegram.

'This is your Uncle Charles' son,' Mother Agata says. 'As you well know, your uncle died shortly after he moved to Chihuahua. At one point, after his death, your father tried to contact his wife and meet their child, but I guess she wasn't interested since she never responded. She must have been afraid that your father might interfere with her life or who knows what. He was about two years younger than you are. I wonder what he'll be like.'

'He arrives on Thursday. Dad was so thrilled because he sent a telegram!'

'Thursday is the thirtieth of May. That is Saint Ferdinand III of Castille's saint's day. The saint of prisoners,' Mother Agata answers.

'I'm actually looking forward to meeting him. It's exciting to actually get to know a lost branch of the family,' Emily says.

'Don't get over-excited. You may be very disappointed. Just think that this young man was raised on a ranch in

Chihuahua!' Mother Agata covers her eyes with her large hands. 'I try to imagine what he looks like and I can't. Who will he look like?'

Mother Agata stands up and shakes her hands as if she were drying them in the air. 'Let's go to the kitchen for some coffee,' she says. 'I don't even know why we even bother to drink coffee in this place. All you have to do is breathe the air and you get coffee straight into your lungs!'

They sit down together at the kitchen table, which is covered with biscuits in the shape of little men and women, like gingerbread men. These are made from baking moulds brought over from Britain by Emily's great-grandmother. On the dough the eyes and hair are drawn with brown icing and the lips are drawn with red icing.

'You can have some of the biscuits, if you like,' Mother Agata says as she hands Emily a small cup of espresso coffee. 'I made over one hundred of them.'

'Should I eat a man or a woman?' Emily asks. 'Now this is always an important decision.'

'I don't know . . .' Mother Agata answers with a grin. Her smile is so large it reminds Emily of a jack-o-lantern face.

'As a child, I always thought that the men and women tasted different. I guess I'll eat the man,' Emily says. First she bites off the arms and then she bites off the legs. 'To think I've been eating these biscuits all my life.'

Mother Agata laughs. 'It's always so interesting to see what people think is important to take with them when they're moving to a foreign country. Your great-grandmother thought that bringing baking moulds to Mexico was important.'

'Well, she brought everything, didn't she? She even brought flower seeds.'

'And one hundred tins of mustard!'

'It feels cruel when you bite the head off,' Emily says as she takes a sip of her coffee and another bite of her biscuit.

Mother Agata covers the biscuits with a linen dishtowel and places the tray under the window. 'Did you read the newspaper today?' Mother Agata asks. 'Did you get a chance to look at it?'

'No, why?' Emily answers as she takes a sip of the dark, bitter coffee.

'There's an interesting article in it about Maria Felix,' Mother Agata says. 'I've clipped it out for you,' she adds as she reaches into the pocket of her white and red chequered apron. 'Here it is,' she says, handing it to Emily.

'You mean the great actress?' Emily asks.

'Yes,' Mother Agata answers. 'You're too young to know, but at one time she was in the papers making news all the time. Everyone always said that she was a man in a woman's body. I think that she was the first woman to smoke cigars in Mexico. Or maybe the only woman to smoke cigars, since I've never seen other women do that.'

'So, what does the newspaper say about her?' Emily asks.

'She had twelve brothers and sisters. As a young girl she

fell in love with her older brother, Pablo. Her parents were so concerned about this relationship that they sent Pablo away to a military school – to separate them.'

'How interesting . . .' Emily says.

'I used to know one of the nuns who taught Maria Felix at the school the actress went to in Guadalajara. The nun said she had once seen her in the park sitting on her brother's lap. She said she saw Maria Felix rub her fingers back and forth inside her brother's mouth, across his teeth.'

'What else does the newspaper say?' Emily asks.

'Maria Felix apparently has admitted that she had an incestuous relationship with her brother. She says that he was her first great love. He died at the military school. To this day nobody knows if he was killed during some rifle exercises or if he committed suicide. Suicides have always been covered up so who knows . . .'

'I remember it perfectly. It was all false. They said she'd killed him in a duel.'

'Oh, of course, I remember now!' Mother Agata exclaims with great enthusiasm, clapping her large hands together. 'They said she had some pistols, or a collection of rare pistols. They got into a terrible fight and she challenged him to a duel. Of course, she knew which of the two pistols had bullets in it.'

While Mother Agata serves Emily some more coffee there is a knock on the kitchen door.

'Come in,' Mother Agata calls out.

The door opens and 'The Japanese' stand in the doorway holding hands. Most of their plaster casts have been removed and only Hipolito still has a cast covering his right leg. They are both very shy with Mother Agata and keep their faces bowed, looking down at the floor.

'Yes, dears, what is it?' Mother Agata asks as she stands up and walks toward the children.

'We would like a glass of water,' Hipolito says as he and Maria tiptoe into the kitchen.

'Of course,' Mother Agata answers. She stands up and takes two glasses down from the cupboard above the sink.

'We don't want two glasses,' Maria says. Emily thinks she looks like she belongs dressed in a kimono and notices that the little girl even shuffles her feet along slowly in tiny steps as if she were actually wearing one.

'We want to drink from the same glass,' Hipolito says.

'Of course,' Mother Agata answers. 'Of course.'

She fills one glass with water and hands it to Hipolito. The children take turns drinking, passing the glass back and forth between them. Emily and Mother Agata watch them in silence. The kitchen is filled with the sound of their little gulping and swallowing noises. When they have finished Maria gives the glass back to Mother Agata.

'Thank you,' they both say in unison as they turn away. Hipolito limps out of the kitchen while Maria holds on to his elbow, helping him walk.

'That water was delicious,' they hear Maria say when she thinks she's out of earshot of the kitchen.

Mother Agata and Emily can hear the sound of Hipolito's cast sliding across the ground as they move down the hall.

Mother Agata sighs.

She places the empty glass in the kitchen sink.

'I should have offered them some biscuits. Oh well . . .' Mother Agata says as she sits back down at the kitchen table. 'I feel tired today. My body feels heavy. My feet feel like two large stones.'

She asks Emily if she will help out by giving one of the orphans an English class. The child is Angelica, a small eleven-year-old girl. Mother Agata knows that the girl is Emily's favourite.

'Of course,' Emily answers. 'I'd be happy to. It's been a few weeks since I spent some time alone with her.'

Emily sits in the inner courtyard with Angelica under the small laurel tree. They are all alone since the other orphans are inside taking other lessons. Angelica hates the sun. She says she will only sit outside for a little while. She also hates lamps and candles. They sit close together but do not touch. Angelica does not like anything to touch her. Angelica is wearing nothing except a white bedsheet wrapped around her body but Emily pretends not to notice.

'I am going to give you an English class today. What do you say to that?' Emily asks.

'I'm happy to take a class from you, Emily,' Angelica answers in a refined, polite tone of voice.

'We'll learn some easy words so just repeat after me: boy.'

Angelica says, 'Boy.'

'Girl.'

Angelica says, 'Girl.'

'Dog.'

Angelica says, 'Dog.'

'Cat.'

Angelica says, 'Cat.'

Emily never likes to teach the orphans the words 'mother' or 'father'.

The orphans are permanently mystified by the fact that Emily does not have a mother but does have a father. They think she is half of what they are. They act as if being left with one parent were somehow impossible. They also find it to be both a beautiful and terrible occurrence. For years they have asked Emily what it feels like to have a father. Ever since Emily was six years old she figured out to tell them that having one parent was like having one arm. The orphans could accept and understand this explanation.

'Emily, I know you're wondering why I'm only wearing this bedsheet, but you're too kind to ask,' Angelica says in a whisper. 'You see, it feels nice and cold. I like how it feels. This is the reason why I am wearing it.'

Angelica hates the sun. She hates light. Anything bright

or shiny hurts. Angelica was burned. She and her family lived in the north of Mexico City, near the Pemex oil refinery. Her father worked as a carpenter and her mother was hired as a part-time seamstress at a nearby clothing factory. One night one of the huge transformers at the refinery exploded, igniting massive vats of gasoline and oil. Whole city blocks around the explosion were destroyed by fire. Dozens of cars and trucks that had been parked in the streets nearby smouldered and burned for weeks.

Angelica was the only member of her family to survive. Pemex, which is owned by the Mexican government, never gave her any help or compensation. After her burns had healed at a government clinic, she lived alone for a few months in the charred remains of her house. She survived by scavenging through rubbish bins on the street and begging at street corners. Mother Agata heard about her and brought her to the orphanage.

'She's the queen of the orphanage,' Mother Agata says. 'No doubt about it, she rules the roost.'

Mother Agata says this because everyone does exactly what Angelica asks. They can't say no to her. 'I think we'd all rob a bank if she asked us to,' Mother Agata adds.

'She's becoming a bit of a tyrant,' Emily says. 'She takes anything she wants – toys and clothes and candy.'

'Yes, but the children feel that their belongings become even more special if Angelica wants them,' Mother Agata answers. 'I know, in my own case, I shouldn't spoil her so much but I just can't help myself. I'm just like the children who are at her beck and call, just the same!'

The girl's face and both arms are badly burned. Two small, black, peppercorn eyes peer out of a face with distorted lips and cheeks. She has no eyebrows or eyelashes. She is missing an ear. She hates the sun. She smells like matches.

As Emily sits beside Angelica on the bench with flashcards of the English words on her lap, she thinks that the girl still smells of burned wire, burned plastic, burned wood, burned bread.

'Repeat again,' Emily says, 'water.'

Angelica says, 'Water.'

'River.'

Angelica says, 'River.'

'Rain.'

Angelica says, 'Rain.'

'Ice.'

Angelica says, 'Ice.'

Mother Agata says, 'If you have been burned, you can grow to love words like ice and rain and river.'

When Emily leaves the orphanage and goes back to her house she finds one red apple on her bed. Snow White's apple.

Fact:
Name: Christine Laverne Slaughter
Born: 12 March 1963, Perry, Florida.
Sentence: Life, eligible for parole in 2007.

She dropped cats from the roof to see if they had nine lives. She decided (after calculating her work in a notebook for several years) that her research proved that most cats only had two or three lives.

Everything hurt her. She said even her hair and fingernails ached. When she put on her clothes they felt painful against her skin. She said that water burned her hands.

Everything grew in her. She said that if someone could look inside her body they would find nails and screws.

She told people that she suffered from snakebites.

In a lapse of two years she went to a hospital fifty times.

Her ailments included the following: she felt her eyes were inside her mouth; her nails were growing backward into her hands; a monkey bit her face; her feet were run over by a train; she heard piano music in her arms; she tasted mint in her ears; her shoulders had been bruised by rain; and an elephant stepped on her arm.

She earned her money by babysitting. The children in her care stopped breathing, were napping, passed out, or fell from their cribs.

When she was caught she had an explanation.

This was her reason:

'The way I done it,

I seen it done on TV shows.

I had my own way,

though. Simple and easy.

No one would hear them

scream.'

7.

Santiago Arrives at Last

Emily does not remember her mother but everyone says she looks just like her. In photographs Emily can see the resemblance. Emily has her mother's straight black hair and light blue eyes. Her skin is so white she can see the veins of her arms and legs as if she looked down into clear water: she sees the pebbles and moss.

Emily's father says that she has an 'Aran Island' face, since this is where her mother grew up, on a small farm on Inishmore. Emily knows that she is not as beautiful as her mother. She knows what nobody says.

'You look like her and you don't,' Mother Agata explains. She quickly changes the subject and tells Emily that her mother slipped into Mexico as if the country were a costume.

'It was quite extraordinary,' Mother Agata says. 'She learned to cook Mexican food and even made tamales from scratch with lard and cornmeal. She used to go around to the markets and learn new recipes from the women who sold their wares. The sad thing was that your father didn't like this food. I think he wanted beef stew. Now that's a joke! They were really opposites in so many ways. On the Day of the Dead she would visit the orphanage and build an altar in the patio covered with flowers, sugar skulls, candles and all kinds of food, including the 'bread of the dead'. Certainly, her favourite day at the orphanage was the sixth of January, Three Kings Day, the Epiphany. She'd have the children write letters to the Magi. Then she'd have them set out their little shoes in the courtyard to receive their gifts. It was lovely. She hated Santa Claus, and so do I for that matter.'

'I have a vague recollection of this,' Emily says.

'I'm sorry, but you cannot remember that.'

'But I do . . .'

'That's impossible. You were just a baby,' Mother Agata protests. 'I think you're confusing memory with what you've been told over the years.'

'But I do remember her . . .'

'She used to dress in the typical Indian dresses from Oaxaca and wear long necklaces of different coloured beads around her neck. Sometimes she'd braid her hair and wrap it around her head like a crown,' Mother Agata says. 'When she dressed like this she looked completely Mexican. Nobody would have guessed that she was Irish. It was uncanny. Sometimes she'd even paint a small black beauty spot on her face. Mexican women used to do that all the time, but you don't see that any more. I also remember that she had a brooch that was a live beetle on a small gold chain. The beetle was covered with pretty coloured stones that had been glued on to the insect's back. I remember that they were very fashionable. You never ever see that any more! See if your father remembers those beetles! Ha! I bet he doesn't! Greta was quite something, when I think about it.'

Emily has her mother's necklaces in a box in her room. In the box there are also rosaries and a fire opal.

'She was like you, in that she was full of facts about all kinds of things. She was very bright. And she particularly loved to read medical dictionaries. She knew all about the functions of the liver and gall bladder. She knew the names of the heart's chambers – things like that. I always thought she probably should have been a medical doctor instead of an architect. Of course she never actually practised as an architect since she came to Mexico to live with your father almost immediately after her graduation. Did you know that within two months her Spanish was remarkable? She already mastered many idioms and slang.'

'She sounds so perfect sometimes,' Emily says. 'It's hard to imagine . . .'

'She was pretty perfect and she was rather wild.'

Emily's father does not talk about her and Emily gets most of her information about her mother from Mother Agata.

'She was always busy running to do this or that. She could never sit still. I thought she wanted to take in the world with one big gulp. When she became a Catholic she calmed down a bit. Just like you, she also liked to have me tell her about the lives of the saints,' Mother Agata explains. 'Whenever she saw me she'd ask what saint's day it was and then ask me to tell her the saint's story.'

Emily's mother's name was Margaret. Everyone called her Greta. Emily knows that there are four saint Margarets: Margaret Clitherow, Margaret Mary, Margaret of Antioch and Margaret of Cortona.

The name Margaret means pearl.

After living in Mexico for two years Emily's mother converted to Catholicism. When she first arrived she went to the Anglican Church that had been founded by the British in 1871.

'Basically she hated anything English,' Mother Agata explains. 'She even made fun of the British community and mocked the people who went to the embassy to celebrate the Queen's birthday. This was hard on your father. He always thought that she became a Catholic to hurt him – or as a complete rejection of his way of life. This just is not true. Your mother told me what really happened.'

One day Emily's mother was in her sewing room hemming some new curtains for the kitchen windows. It was early in the morning and nobody was home. Emily's mother heard the soft voice of a woman whisper to her. The voice said 'console' and 'heed'.

'Your mother said she thought that those were the two most beautiful words she had ever heard in her life. It was like a visitation. She even looked around, thinking there was someone in the room with her,' Mother Agata says. 'It was true. The words changed her. They had a calming effect on her. Those words turned her around. She said that she knew that it was Mary who was speaking.'

In the box of Emily's mother's belongings there are three rosaries: one is made of silver, one is made of white grey seeds, and the third is made of green glass beads.

'She always carried a rosary in her pocket,' Mother Agata adds, 'or wrapped around her wrist. She said the beads warmed her skin and not the other way around. I remember she'd often go and visit the Black Christ in the Metropolitan Cathedral.'

'You took me to see it when I was a child. Don't you remember?' Emily asks.

'Of course. Everything you know is thanks to me,' Mother Agata says and smiles.

'Yes,' Emily answers. She leans toward Mother Agata and kisses her cheek.

'Your mother used to tell me that she felt like one of those drawings that hang in butchers' shops.'

'Which drawings?'

'You know, the one of a cow divided up into pieces, which show all the different cuts of meat. She said she felt just like that: her legs were Irish, her face was Catholic, her arms were Mexican, her heart belonged to you.'

'I miss her so much and I didn't even know her. Why

did that happen? How can you miss someone you never knew?'

'I remember one funny story or, rather, one thing she said. I am sure I already told this to you. She once came to me and told me that since I was the head of the orphanage and a Mother Superior that she was going to give me some "mother's advice". She said it was called "mother's advice" since this counsel had been passed down through the mothers in her family for generations.'

'Really?' Emily says with astonishment. 'I don't think you've ever told me this. And what is it?'

'Your mother told me that "mother's advice" was to know that there were some things that were worth killing for and going to jail for.'

'What things?'

'She said being lied to or spat on.'

'Being lied to or spat on?'

'Yes. I do think there is some truth to it. I've never been spat on, but it must feel terrible.'

Fact:

Charlene Gallego was born in 1956 and was a certified genius. Her IQ tests registered at 160. She could add up, subtract, multiply and divide any number.

Charlene met Gerald Gallego, her third husband, at a poker club in Sacramento. 'I thought he was a very nice, clean-cut fellow,' Charlene said years later. He liked it that she was quick with numbers. She could calculate the numbers that were left in a deck of cards after certain cards had been played. Playing cards, they always beat everyone.

Charlene liked the number seven.

Seven is a sacred number.

3 + 4

2 + 5

1 + 6

are the sums of numbers from the opposite sides of a die.

When she added up the people they had killed the sum was seven lives.

Charlene later explained, 'I mean, like it was easy and fun and we really enjoyed it, so why shouldn't we do it?'

8.

The Key Won't Unlock the Door

In the evening, when Emily arrives home from the orphanage and opens the front door, the sounds of men's voices reach her as she enters the front hall. She hangs her coat on a row of brass hooks nailed to the wall beside the front door and notices what is obviously her cousin's very worn, brown leather jacket hanging there also.

Emily follows the voices down the hall and into the library. Beside the unlit fireplace she sees her father kneeling on the floor with her cousin Santiago kneeling beside him. They are having a cup of coffee and are bent over Emily's father's collection of white butterflies laid out on the deep red Persian carpet. The butterflies, which are pinned to large swatches of green felt cloth, look like dozens of torn pieces of white paper.

'Ah, here is Emily,' Emily's father says as she walks into the library. 'Darling,' he continues, 'this is your cousin, Santi. I've just been showing him my collection of white butterflies. He'll be staying with us while he looks for a job and gets settled. I've given him your mother's old sewing room to stay in. What do you think?'

Santi turns away from the table and faces Emily and smiles at her. He stands slightly hunched over to one side with his hands in the pockets of his blue jeans. She looks into his face as if she gazed into a mirror, to see if he looks at all like her – in search of some feature that shows the bloodline. She thinks that he does not look like he belongs in the family. Santiago is tall, like everyone on Emily's father's side, but his Spanish, British, Mexican Indian blood is forged by history: pyramids, galleons, Vikings. He has long black hair that curls at the base of his neck, and black eyes. His dark skin is covered with darker freckles.

Emily reaches out to shake his hand but he keeps his hands inside his pockets, takes a step toward her and kisses her cheek.

'It is nice to meet you,' Santi says. His English has a soft Spanish accent, which fills and elongates every vowel. As she stands beside him she thinks she can smell the scent of someone who has lived in the desert – dry grass and gravel.

'He's an architect, like your mother was. He studied in Monterrey,' Emily's father explains. 'He says he wanted to study abroad, but in Mexico you can study architecture right after finishing preparatory, which made him decide to stay. He was also explaining that he finished school at age sixteen with honours. Isn't this remarkable? You did say honours, am I correct?'

'Yes,' Santiago replies and takes his hands out of his pockets and picks up his coffee cup. Emily notices that even his hands, like his face, are covered with the dark spots of pigment. 'I've always liked to build things, even as a child. Once I built a whole city with pebbles and stones. Actually, I was just telling your father that there is more work for architects here than there is in Chihuahua, which is why I've come to Mexico City.'

'Your saint is Saint Barbara then,' Emily answers automatically. 'Sorry,' she adds a little embarrassed. 'You see, I'm writing a paper on saints for a class at the university, so they are very much on my mind. She's the patron saint of architects . . .'

'Emily knows all about saints,' her father interrupts and gestures for everyone to sit down. 'It is quite a feat! Do you want a cup of coffee, Em?' he adds.

'Really? But do you actually believe in them?' Santi asks. 'These things are more like superstitions, don't you think?'

'Some people say they have seen Saint Barbara appear in the contour of bricks and stone and even reflected in glass windowpanes,' Emily answers. 'If you look hard enough, you might just find her . . . or so they say . . .'

'Well, I'll look for her now that I know,' Santi says, taking a sip of coffee. 'They didn't teach me these things when I studied architecture!'

'Strange as it may sound, and everything to do with saints is strange, Saint Barbara is also the saint of miners,' Emily adds. 'Miners never like to build things; they only like to quarry, burrow and dig tunnels.'

'In our family I think we always worshipped silver. No one looked to grow vegetables in the soil, we just looked at the ground as a place to dig for treasure,' Emily's father says. 'Emily is going to do her thesis on the cult of saints and how these cults have affected certain societies,' Emily's father says. 'She's getting her masters degree in history.'

'How interesting,' Santi answers. 'I don't know anything about saints.'

'Well, you obviously weren't raised by Mother Agata, as I was. She's the director of our orphanage, the one that was founded by our family – the Rosa of Lima Orphanage,' Emily answers. 'We continue to be affected by the lives of the saints and some of our superstitions are founded on things that have to do with their lives. Some saints even have their own personal emblems. I suppose that this is like a kind of heraldry.'

Emily serves herself a cup of coffee and sits down beside Santi and her father around the unlit fireplace. Her father folds away his cloths filled with butterflies.

'You both speak English so perfectly. Do you ever speak Spanish?' Santi asks as he leans back into the worn armchair that is covered in a dark red brocade fabric. 'My father and mother always spoke Spanish to me; although my mother did give me English lessons. I guess it's a bit ridiculous to be called Santiago Neale and to speak English the way I do.'

'Your English is fine,' Emily's father answers. 'It would be just like my brother Charles to speak to you in Spanish. He always said he was born in Mexico and, therefore, he was Mexican. We had different points of view on all of this. I never felt that one excluded the other. The fact is Charles did call you Santiago and not James, which would be the English equivalent.'

As Santi listens to Emily's father speak he raps his fingers on his knees as if they were a piano. There is a melody in the tapping, as though his fingers were following music that he was hearing in his head.

'Do you play the piano?' Emily asks as she looks at his fingers move with great dexterity.

'No, I play the accordion,' Santi answers. 'This is a habit that I have. It keeps my fingers flexible.'

'He's brought it with him,' Emily's father says. 'I told him we'd like to hear him play one of these days. It seems like years since I heard an accordion. Can you play a polka?'

'My father traded a horse for my accordion at a state fair. Can you believe it? These are things that still happen in the provinces. I basically taught myself how to play. And, yes, of course I can play a polka, although I have to admit that I am not very fond of polkas.'

Outside they hear the loud whistle of the man who sells steaming sweet potatoes from a cart on wheels.

'Santiago,' Emily's father says, 'May I ask why on earth did you send us a telegram? We've been wondering about this, haven't we, Em?'

'My father told me that you loved telegrams. Sometimes he'd talk to me about you and his childhood. He said that as a boy you wanted to have a bicycle and be a telegram delivery boy, so I thought it would be something fun to do.'

Emily's father looks at Santi in amazement. 'What odd turns and twists . . .' he says.

During the course of the evening, Santiago tells them about his life growing up on a small farm in Chihuahua. His father died when he was very young and then Santi and his mother lived alone on the farm for years. His mother died when he was seventeen. He was already in Monterrey at that time. 'I hated to sell the farm,' Santi says. 'When you sell something it means that you can never return, you can never go back. I always think that some day I may be able to buy it back. Perhaps everyone thinks this when they get rid of something. That place is so full of memories and both my parents are buried there.'

'Who bought it?' Emily asks.

'A family from Tijuana,' Santi answers. 'I suspect that they may have been drug dealers since they paid for it in cash. They actually arrived with plastic supermarket bags filled with paper money. What could I do? It's not easy to sell a ranch in the middle of nowhere.'

'This house used to have a great deal of land surrounding

it, but pieces were sold off in the 1920s and then again in the 1940s, after the war,' Emily's father explains. 'We used to have lemon and apple trees and two enormous avocado trees.'

Outside they hear the short whistle of the man on a bicycle, who sells bread from an enormous, flat basket attached to the bicycle's handlebars.

'That whistle. What is that?' Santi asks. He stands up and walks toward the window that looks out on the street.

'The man who sells bread,' Emily answers.

'Excellent. We'll have to buy some one of these days. I love fresh bread.'

'Yes, of course,' Emily answers.

'Actually, except for the surrounding land, the house itself is pretty untouched,' Emily's father continues. 'Many of the things that we have were brought over on a ship by my grandfather. The books in the library were his too.'

'My grandfather also,' Santi replies without hesitation. 'Well, he would have been my great-grandfather,' he adds.

There is a short, uneasy silence as Emily and her father stare at Santi. He stands up, picks up the tray with the empty coffee cups and walks confidently to the kitchen. Emily picks up the coffee pot and sugar bowl and she and her father follow Santi into the kitchen. Emily thinks that he moves as if he had lived in the house before and knows where to find things.

'Yes, yes, of course,' Emily stammers. 'That is what my father meant. I'll have to show you all the books and things.'

She watches Santi as he washes his hands in the kitchen sink.

'I'm so sorry. It is going to take me a little bit of time to get used to having a new member of the family around here . . .' Emily's father adds. 'I'll have to tell you stories about our family and the mines. Emily loves to hear the stories of how the miners used to steal the silver. They hollowed out the handles of their hammers or concealed grains of silver and gold in their mouth, teeth and ears. One famous story is about an overseer who was killed in an accident. He was disembowelled and filled with silver before being removed from the mine. They were fascinating times . . .'

Emily watches as Santi opens a kitchen drawer and takes out a washcloth to dry his hands.

'I am quite tired,' Santi says abruptly as he hangs the cloth over the back of a kitchen chair. 'It has been a long day for me. I think I'll go to bed now. Goodnight.'

'Goodnight,' Emily answers. 'Don't you want some supper?'

'No, thank you. I'm quite sleepy.'

'Let us know if you need anything,' Emily's father says as Santi walks out of the kitchen.

'Yes, thank you so much,' Santi answers and pauses under the doorframe. 'Oh, by the way,' he says, 'I have heard about Mother Agata. My parents told me about her and about the orphanage,' he adds as he turns around and leaves the room.

Emily and her father sit down at the kitchen table. They listen to the sound of Santi's footsteps going up the stairs.

'He seems very nice,' Emily's father says after a short while.

'Yes,' Emily answers. 'Although it is strange to have someone else staying here. Did he mention why he never contacted you before or why his family lost touch with ours?'

'No,' Emily's father answers, taking off his glasses and rubbing his eyes with the backs of his hands. 'I didn't want to get into that. He'll talk about it when he feels like it. He reminds me of my brother. I feel as if my brother had walked into this house. Do you know that I'm sure that leather jacket he was wearing belonged to my brother? I recognised it instantly.'

'Really?'

Emily's father stands up and looks straight at Emily, 'I feel as if I've been sitting with a ghost all night,' he says and, in quick strides, leaves and goes up the stairs to his bedroom.

Emily closes the curtains and turns off the lamps. She walks to the kitchen, drinks a glass of water and then goes up the stairs and walks along the corridor past her mother's sewing room where Santi is staying. The door is closed but she can hear music inside. She hears the muted sound of Jimi Hendrix:

> There's a red house over yonder
> that's where my baby stays
> Lord, there's a red house over yonder
> Lord, that's where my baby stays . . .

When Emily enters her bedroom, she finds a yellow pencil lying on her pillow. She picks it up and looks at it closely. The end of the pencil is embedded with small dents: tooth marks. Santi's music follows her into her room:

There's a red house over yonder
that's where my baby stays

The bedroom window, which looks out over the street, is wide open. A cool breeze enters the room. A few moist and bruised flowers from the jacaranda tree outside have been blown into her room. She leans over and picks up the blossoms and presses them into one hand. She squeezes the milky sap into her palm.

Emily looks out the window. The street is empty except for a tall man dressed in a long, beige raincoat, who is walking a black poodle down the street. He moves with his head bent to one side as he smokes on a cigarette. People in the neighbourhood say he is a poet.

Emily closes the window and sits on her bed. She can hear the faded sound of her father's romantic music downstairs; a song by Agustin Lara mixes with Santi's music that continues to play in the sewing room down the hall:

Wait a minute, something's wrong here
the key won't unlock the door

wait a minute, something's wrong

Lord, have mercy, this key won't unlock the

door . . .

As Emily holds the pencil in her hand she rubs her thumb over the dented tooth marks. She thinks of how there is a saint for pencils.

Fact:

She was born Brynhild Paulsdatter Storset in 1859, but everyone called her 'Belle'.

She hired drifters to work on her farm. She placed 'lonely hearts' ads in newspapers. The advertisements said, 'A real Belle is looking for a real Beau.'

Any man who came near to her was never seen again.

Strychnine is a poison. It is also called dog button, mole-nots and mole death. It has no colour and is a crystalline powder with a bitter taste. Strychnine is a component of the dog button plant and has fruits that resemble small oranges. The seeds of these fruits contain the most poison. When they are ingested, the first symptoms are a stiff neck and face. The blossoms of the plant smell like curry powder.

Poems were written about her:

> *There's red upon the Hoosier moon*
> *For Belle was strong and full of doom;*
> *And think of all those Norka men*
> *Who'll never see St Paul again.*

She said that if you kill someone that person gets inside of you. You will feel their arms in your arms, their legs in your legs. So she became strong like the men she'd killed.

She asked people to touch the muscles of her arms.

She could carry anything.

Some people said she could lift a horse and hold it up above her head.

9.

When 'The Japanese' Become Echoes

Mexico City has three names. When it is ancient and sad it is known as *Mexico Tenochtitlan;* when it is beautiful in the afternoon psychedelic light of bougainvilleas it is called 'Mexico'; and when it is a modern, overpopulated shriek it is called the 'Federal District'. When addressing a letter, the simple abbreviation 'DF' is all that is required for identifying the metropolis.

In Mexico City the sky is brown smoke. The sky is yellow smoke. The sky is green smoke. The sky no longer belongs to heaven. It is not a sky. It is a ceiling.

On the way to the orphanage from the university Emily drives along the long interior highway that snakes throughout the city. She looks at the enormous wall-like billboards. One shows an open mouth exposing a tongue and tonsils; advertising dental procedures. These are structures of massive images: a woman smiles in an advertisement for a department store; television stations promote soap operas;

political parties introduce their candidates. There are also large advertisements for Pepsi, pre-packaged flour tortillas, Volkswagen and Alka-Seltzer.

Emily drives past a dog that was killed on the road, she looks away and swerves so her tyres do not touch the blood and gore.

There is so much traffic that the cars barely move. Because of this, the highway becomes a market. Between the lanes vendors sell newspapers, sweets and cigarettes, bottles of water, Japanese peanuts, and flowers. Sometimes they sell small bouquets of pearl-white gardenias tied in transparent cellophane.

As Emily moves slowly along the road she looks at the people in the cars that surround her. Several women apply make-up on their faces using the car's rearview mirror; one man shaves with a battery-operated electric razor, a few people read the newspaper; but the majority look as if they are about to fall asleep.

Today the city is the *Distrito Federal*: a modern, overpopulated shriek.

Emily turns on the radio. A traditional Mexican children's song is playing:

> *The White Lady is covered*
> *With pillars of gold and silver;*
> *Let us break down a pillar*
> *To see the White Lady.*

When Emily arrives at the orphanage she spends a few minutes in the car looking at the building from outside. The walls are painted rust red and the long French windows that open onto the street are painted with a band of dark blue that frames each window. A bougainvillea of yellowish-white flowers grows along the side of one wall. The front door is a massive palatial entryway of solid, overly varnished oak. The shiny brass knocker on the door has been crafted from ancient moulds that made the knockers look like hands.

Emily thinks about all the orphans that must have stood at that door and looked at that brass hand.

She gets out of the car and walks to the entrance and knocks, holding the brass hand in her hand. The door opens immediately since 'The Japanese' have been waiting for her arrival and have stood behind the door at several intervals for most of the morning. They hold hands and jump up and down when they see her walk in.

'You're supposed to ask who it is before you open a door,' Emily scolds. 'What if I were a thief?'

'Mother Agata is sick. Mother Agata is in bed,' they say in a chorus of voices that are like small brass chimes. Emily thinks that they are beginning to behave as if they were one person.

'What do you mean by sick? What's wrong?'

'We don't know,' Maria answers. 'She's in her room and nobody is here. No other nun or teacher. We're all alone and she's sick.'

For the orphans it is always terrifying when Mother Agata is unwell. They are scared of further loss. Mother Agata's illness makes all the children in the orphanage react in different ways. Some fall asleep and some hug each other or walk around holding hands.

Hipolito says that Angelica has been hiding under her bed all morning. It is her favourite place: cool and dark. 'She didn't even come out for breakfast and she didn't want to speak to anyone.'

Emily walks across the inner courtyard, which is cluttered with all kinds of stuffed animals, tricycles, building blocks and an assortment of plastic dolls, to Mother Agata's room. 'It's me,' Emily whispers outside the door. 'May I come in?' she asks again as she softly raps her knuckles on the door.

Mother Agata calls out, 'Yes, yes, come in.'

Emily opens the door and sees Mother Agata sitting in an armchair reading the newspaper.

'Oh, it is you,' Mother Agata says. 'Thank God. The children will simply not leave me alone!'

'What's the matter?' Emily asks, '"The Japanese" told me you were ill.'

'Oh, it is nothing,' Mother Agata says as she closes the newspaper and points at her chest. 'It is just a bad cold.'

Boxes of tissues surround Mother Agata and there is a cup of tea and a jar of honey on a tray by her oversized bed. She is sitting in an armchair that is too small for her, but she is used to making herself fit into tight spaces. Her grey hair falls loosely around her shoulders.

It is always a shock for Emily to see Mother Agata without her nun's habit on. She looks so ordinary, so human, like an old aunt. Emily thinks that when Mother Agata is dressed like a nun she seems like an angel, a shaman, a witch – otherworldly.

'I should be up and about by tomorrow. You know I especially don't want Angelica to catch this since she has no defences whatsoever,' Mother Agata says, reaching for the tea and taking a long sip of the liquid.

Emily notices that there are two large tortoiseshell hair-combs on Mother Agata's bedside table. They lie next to a photograph of Mother Agata with some of the orphans.

'Your mother gave them to me,' Mother Agata says, following Emily's gaze. 'She said she wanted me to own something feminine and beautiful.'

'How nice,' Emily answers. She picks them up and looks at them closely. 'They look old.'

'Yes, I think they're very old. She bought them in an antique store. They were probably Spanish.'

Emily sits down on the armrest of Mother Agata's armchair, 'Is there anything you need? Is there anything I can do for you?'

'No, thank you. I'm fine. I just have to stay in bed for a few days. But, tell me, I've been very worried about you. Have strange things continued to happen in the house. Have you noticed anything else? Has anything been moved?'

'No,' Emily answers. 'I think I must have imagined it all. Maybe I was distracted.' She places the combs in Mother Agata's hair. 'These combs look beautiful in your hair,' Emily says. 'No, nothing else has happened. The house is fine. I'm fine. I must have imagined it all,' she adds.

'By the way,' Mother Agata asks, 'did you read the newspaper today? I just read the most extraordinary thing. Listen.'

Mother Agata picks up the newspaper and turns the pages. 'Here it is,' she says. 'I'll read it to you.'

She clears her throat, blows her nose and begins to read, 'It says: A brother and a sister, Reina and Carlos Martinez, lived together in the Roma neighbourhood. They never married and had lived with their mother their whole lives. After their mother's death they turned off the heat and gas and used kerosene lamps or candles and went without running water. Reina could be seen running around the neighbourhood in a tattered yellow bathrobe shopping for food or carrying loads of junk that she found in the streets. She had a supermarket cart that she used for wheeling everything back to the house. Often she was seen looking through other people's trash that had been left outside on the sidewalk. Once she was seen carrying an old mattress on her back.

'Then a bad odour began to emanate from the house and there suddenly seemed to be many more cats around than before. The police went into the residence after receiving a call from the neighbours. They tried to get in for several hours and finally had to call the fire department, who used a ladder to enter through one of the windows. Inside the police found that it was not possible to even walk around because of the vast accumulation of objects. The excavation project continued for weeks and trucks had to be brought in to clear everything away.

'In the house they found fourteen pianos, stacks of newspapers, sewing machines, a baby carriage, the chassis from a Model T Ford, six stoves, three refrigerators, eighteen tyres, three violins, four bicycles, dozens of socks filled with coins, hundreds of empty milk cartons, a stuffed owl, piles and piles of shoes, and more.

'The decomposed bodies of Reina and Carlos were found two weeks later in one of the back rooms. Carlos was lying on the floor holding a rotten apple in one hand. The authorities suspect he was carrying it to feed his sick sister. Reina was lying in a bed surrounded by dolls and parts of dolls – pink plastic legs, heads, and hands, which she had obviously found in rubbish bins throughout the city. The authorities say that they have not found a will and that there appears to be no heirs. Their bank statement shows a balance of over four million pesos.'

'That's incredible!' Emily exclaims. 'They were collectors. True collectors. The real thing!'

'When you walk down a street you never know what is happening behind all those closed doors,' Mother Agata says placing the newspaper down on the floor beside her. 'Everyone has a secret life, I suppose. I've often wondered what would happen if everyone had to live with their doors and windows open. If we could see inside each other's homes, would we behave differently?'

'So, tell me,' Mother Agata asks and takes another sip from her cup of tea. 'What about Santiago? Did he come? Wasn't he supposed to arrive yesterday?'

'Yes,' Emily answers. 'He was there with Dad when I got home last night. Dad was showing him his collection of white butterflies, of course. He thinks everyone should like his butterflies and insects as much as he does.'

'So, what's he like?'

'He's an orphan, but we knew that,' Emily answers. 'My father says he reminds him of his brother Charles.'

'Since he is an orphan he'll be coming over to visit us for sure.'

'I don't know,' Emily replies. 'He's a grown-up and so it is different.'

'Emily,' Mother Agata says, taking a sip of her tea, 'it is never different. I've seen this time and time again. There is only one thing worse and that is when a child dies and the mother or father becomes the orphan of their child. You're mother used to say this. To be the orphan of your child is the greatest tragedy on earth. Your mother used to say that there should be orphanages for the parents of lost children.'

'Well, like my mother, Santiago is an architect. He just

finished his studies at a university in Monterrey. I guess he's very bright since he graduated from preparatory school at a really young age. He's going to live with us for a while until he finds a job. My father seems pleased, which is odd since he never likes company.'

'He's probably making an exception for you so that you can have some family. I look forward to meeting him,' Mother Agata answers. 'By the way,' she adds, sitting up straight in the small armchair, 'I've been meaning to ask you. How are "The Japanese"? How do you think they're adapting?'

'They seem fine. Perhaps they could be a bit more independent of one another. We could nudge them toward a few activities that they can't share. Why do you ask? Is there something you've noticed?'

'Yes, as a matter of fact I have noticed something,' Mother Agata answers. 'You see, they've become echoes. They just repeat everything the other one says. What do we do?'

'They've become echoes. They've become echoes,' Emily repeats to herself.

As Emily leaves the orphanage she sees 'The Japanese' squatting under a eucalyptus tree. They are bent over and stare intently at something on the ground around their feet. Their heads touch.

'What are you two looking at?' Emily asks, walking over to them. She can smell the musty mint of the tree's leaves and bark as she stands beneath it. She sees that the ground is covered with the small, round eucalyptus cones. She picks one up and holds it in her left hand.

'Go away,' Hipolito says, waving one of his hands toward her. 'We are doing something.'

'Go away,' Maria says. 'We are doing something.'

'But what is it?' Emily asks again.

'Not much. Nothing at all,' Maria says.

'Not much. Nothing at all,' Hipolito repeats.

Maria looks up at Emily. Emily can see that her eyes are filled with tears.

'We are spitting on ants to see if they can swim,' Maria says.

Fact:

willful blind·ness, noun. Deliberate failure to make a reasonable inquiry of wrongdoing (as drug dealing in one's house) despite suspicion or an awareness of the high probability of its existence
NOTE: Willful blindness involves conscious avoidance of the truth and gives rise to an inference of knowledge of the crime in question.

(Merriam-Webster's Dictionary of Law)

Locusta was a professional killer who lived during the first century AD. She is the first documented serial killer. In the year 54 AD, the Empress Agrippina hired Locusta to poison Emperor Claudius and Britannicus (Claudius's 14-year-old son from a previous marriage).

Locusta of Gaul knew how to prepare poisonous mushrooms. She dried them, crushed them into powders and sprinkled them into drinks or cooked them into soups and sauces.

She tested their toxicity on animals.

Death Cap (Amanita phalloides), Fool's Mushroom (A. verna), Destroying Angel or Death Angel (A. virosa) and Smaller Death Angel (A. bisporiger) are the names of poisonous mushrooms.

The poison in the fungi is amanitin and phalloidin.

Locusta was blind when she closed her eyes.

10.

In Defence of Wolves

Two people living in a house makes a home very quiet. Three people living in a house create a lot of sound and commotion. For the first time Emily comprehends that the sounds of the street and the sounds of objects within the house had always surrounded her. She no longer hears the wood furniture creak and everything seems a little out of place. Santi's books, jackets and sweaters, shoes, and his objects like rulers and pencils, lie around as if the whole house were his. The kitchen is filled with platters of light green grapes that he buys in the market.

Since Santi's arrival a few days ago, Emily and her father spend their evenings sitting with him in the kitchen or in the library. They drink coffee with hot milk or have a couple of shot glasses of tequila.

In Chihuahua Santi lived on a cattle ranch close to the Conchos River and the town of Bocoyna. 'Try to imagine living in an environment where everything is hot. The walls, the ground, your shoes, the water and, well, just everything was warm. You can't understand it unless you've lived it. I find I am constantly touching the walls here since I can't get used to how cool they feel. I like walking barefoot on the stone floors.'

From his father's land Santi says he could see the railway tracks that led from Mexico's border with the United States through Chihuahua and down to Los Mochis in Sinaloa.

'That railway track was like a long river,' Santi says. 'Everyone followed it, everything happened on it. I remember seeing boxcars filled with sugar going north to Texas. There was always some container that leaked so the train tracks would get sprinkled with grains of sugar. Then a few dozen desert mice and rabbits would appear out of nowhere to lick the sugar off of the ties. People lived, died and even gave birth on those tracks,' Santi explains. 'Women would lay out their laundry on the rails for it to dry. Wild animals and an occasional drunk would get killed by a train. Then the buzzards would come.'

'I remember seeing buzzards in Mexico City also. It wasn't common, but occasionally you would see one. Now you never do,' Emily's father adds.

'I've never seen one,' Emily says. 'I've only seen one in an encyclopaedia.'

Santi explains that as a child he liked to stand as close as he could get to the trains and feel their wind and speed and listen to the crunch of gravel and wheeze of the wheels.

'I always wanted to ride on one of those trains but I never did,' Santi says, shaking his head. 'There are no passenger trains any more. Back then, many people would try to hide in them in order to get to the Mexico/United States border. Sometimes you could see their faces peeking out between spaces in the doors. They were like spectres. Some, who were very brave, rode the exterior ladders. This was my world.'

Santi did not go to school in Bocoyna until he was ten years old. He knows how to ride horses, lasso cattle, weave baskets and play the accordion.

Some evenings he plays the accordion for Emily and her father. He sits in a stiff kitchen chair with the instrument between his legs and his head bent over as if he were whispering to the instrument. He cups the bellows' strap around one wrist, hits the buttons and pulls the bellows in and out.

Emily's father is impressed that Santi knows Lara's songs. 'He was a poet. He was even called "the singing poet". Everyone used to know his songs by heart,' Emily's father says.

As Santi plays, Emily's father mouths the words:

> *With tears of blood you can write the story*
> *of the sacred sainted love*
> *that you gave birth to.*
> *With tears of blood you can buy glory*
> *and turn it into verses*
> *and place them at your feet.*

Santi can also play songs from the north of Mexico, and tangos.

Emily's father stands up and opens a drawer in one of the kitchen's cabinets. He takes out six small silver teaspoons. 'Santiago, these were the first things that were made when your great-grandfather discovered that small silver vein,' he says as he lays the spoons on the table in front of Santi. 'It seems to me that you should have some of these. They are a part of your history too. Can you see the letter "N" engraved in the silver? Mexican silversmiths have always been the best.'

'Thank you,' Santi answers and places two spoons to one side.

When Emily's father talks about everything that has disappeared, Santi tells them about the farm.

'So many things disappeared there also,' Santi says. 'Even sounds. It is not just Mexico City, it happens everywhere. When I was about ten years old, the trains stopped passing by. Even though we knew they would not be coming any longer we could not help but listen for them, especially at night. I can still hear the phantom trains inside of me. Only a person who has lived near trains can understand this. I still hear them in me and feel their movement. I always think that one of the saddest sights is an abandoned train track.'

'The phantom trains. Yes, I can understand that,' Emily's father answers.

Santi adds that as a child he saw grey wolves, rattlesnakes and porcupines. Once in a while wild turkeys could be seen walking in the middle of the railway tracks, looking for the dry corn that fell from the trains' boxcars.

He remembers how the owner of one farm, who lived a few kilometres down the road, was so proud of the three grey wolves he had killed that he had them stuffed and placed on his porch so everyone could see them.

'The man thought his wolves were funny. He even placed cigars in the wolves' maws,' Santi says, biting his lower lip. He picks up one of the sliver spoons and rubs his thumb over the spoon's back, inside, and around the rim.

'Of course there aren't any wolves left in Mexico. Those were probably the last wolves ever to roam the State of Chihuahua.'

Santi is sure this man must have been an important drug dealer, since he also owned a fleet of a dozen cars with darkened windows.

'This man's great dream in life was to go to Africa and kill a lion,' Santi explains. 'He always began his conversations by saying: when I go to Africa . . .'

'Did you ever go to cock fights?' Emily's father asks Santiago.

'No, although I know they occurred all over the place. I remember that people used to say that there were dogfights held in the desert, but I don't know. Everything of mystery and evil happened "out in the desert". You can't find anyone out there. The desert is a perfect place for committing crimes.'

'Did you hear of any of these crimes?' Emily asks.

'There were always rumours about people disappearing. What I do remember is seeing Tarahumara Indians every so often, maybe once every two years. They were generally from the region of Nararachic and they were peyote-seekers. They came to find the plants in the desert. I never tried peyote. Too many people go crazy doing that. But we did use it as a poultice. Peyote is good for snakebites, burns, and wounds of any kind. My mother always kept some on a shelf in the kitchen.'

One night Santi tells Emily and her father about the remains of an ancient mammoth they found on the ranch. Emily, Santi and Emily's father sit in the library drinking shots of tequila chased with beer.

'My father had been digging up the north corner of the farm to plant some alfalfa when he discovered the bones,' Santi explains. 'I helped him dig them out. It must have been a mature animal since the tusks were enormous. At the site we also found spears and flint arrowheads. My father wanted to notify the National Institute of Anthropology, but my mother wouldn't allow it. She said she didn't want anyone from the Mexican government stepping on her land.'

'That could have been an important archaeological find,' Emily says. 'Wasn't there some way to tell someone privately or at least preserve the site?'

Santi sighs and continues, 'There was nothing my mother disliked more than the Mexican government. She said that anytime she met a politician she wanted to spit.'

Emily's father says that he feels the same way. He cannot get anyone to care about the disappearance of butterflies and beetles.

'Nobody cares. I write letters to senators and I even published a few articles in magazines, but nobody cares,' Emily's father says as he rubs his head with his fingers. 'One year ago a neighbour cut down a large beautiful jacaranda tree because he said it was messy. Imagine, he thought that the dry flowers were rubbish! In ten minutes he cut down a tree that took one hundred years or more to grow! This man is the son of a medical doctor at one of the city's top hospitals! So, tell me, what hope is there?'

'What happened to the mammoth?' Emily asks. 'Was it just left there?'

'Yes. Maybe it's still there,' Santi answers. 'We never did anything with it. We never told anyone. I kept the arrowheads, though. The bones are probably gone. The desert destroys everything,' Santi says in a whisper and repeats again, 'The desert destroys everything.'

Emily's father stretches his hands above his head. He slowly stands, holding his hip with his hand. 'I'm getting too old to stay up so late drinking. I'll see you in the morning.' He places his empty shot glass on the table and walks slowly out of the room.

After a little while, Emily turns to look at Santi. 'He's getting old. Sometimes it is hard to watch,' she says.

Santi does not answer. Instead, he leans over and picks up the accordion that lies at his feet and hooks it around his wrist in a quick, rhythmic gesture. 'I'll see you in the morning,' he says and leaves the room in two quick strides.

Emily stands up and tidies the library. She takes the glasses to the kitchen. She turns out the lights, walks to the front door and locks it with the key and a large, old iron bolt, which her great-grandfather had placed on the door during the Mexican Revolution.

When she goes up to her room, Emily sits on the bed and takes off her blouse. She leans over to turn on the lamp and, as she reaches for the switch, she sees a small grey arrowhead on her bedside table.

She thinks about:
the pillow on the floor,
dress on her bed,
drawers pulled open,
a red apple,
the chewed up pencil on her pillow.

Emily can feel her heart beating in her wrists. She can taste dry desert dust in her mouth. She can hear people outside walking in the street. She can hear a woman say, 'There has been no rain for four weeks.'

She can smell the carrion.

Fact:
Susan 'Sadie' Atkins is prisoner number WO8304 at California Institution for Women at Frontera.

She said at one parole hearing, 'I don't have to just make amends to the victims and families, I have to make amends to society. I sinned against God and everything this country stands for.'

The name Susan means 'Lily'.

Patricia 'Katie' Krenwrinckel is prisoner number W08314 at California Institution for Women at Frontera.

The name Patricia means 'of noble birth'.

Leslie Van Houten is prisoner number W13378 at California Institution for Women at Frontera.

Van Houten told the parole board, 'My heart aches and there seems to be no way to convey the amount of pain I caused. I don't know what else to say.'

The name Leslie means 'of the grey fortress'.

They do not know how to write with pencils or pens.
They write with their fingers dipped in blood.
They can draw straight lines and perfect circles.
They do not write this word: Mercy.

They can walk like soldiers.
One, two, three, four, five.
If a man tells them to march, they march.
One, two, three, four, five.
They can take orders.
One, two, three, four, five.
They can write words on their foreheads.
One, two, three, four, five.

II.

The Arrowhead

Emily sits on the edge of her bed. She holds the arrowhead in her hand and moves it around in her palm under the lamplight. It still feels warm from the desert. She studies the chips and cuts that have chiselled it into a weapon and imagines the arrowhead embedded deep in the Mammoth's ribs. She knows it was once covered in the animal's ancient blood.

After twenty minutes, Emily stands up. She puts her blouse back on, picks up the arrowhead and marches down to Santi's room in six quick, broad steps. She stands outside, takes in a deep breath and knocks on the door. In an instant she hears Santi call out, 'Come in.'

Emily walks into the room. It is her mother's sewing room and nothing there has been changed or moved since her mother disappeared. The sewing machine is in one corner beside a long, standing mirror. On one table there is a basket filled with spools of thread in dozens of different colours. On the wall there are six pegs where her mother's straw and wool hats still hang. On another wall there is an old and faded print of Bonnard's painting of a woman lying in a bathtub. Emily knows that inside the small, narrow closet her mother's raincoat still hangs. The garment holds tissues in one of its pockets.

Santi is lying on the small day bed and is under the covers. Emily walks in and stands in front of him. She stretches out her arm and opens her fist and shows him the arrowhead in her hand. She does not say a word.

Santi smiles. 'It is about time you put two and two together. I was beginning to wonder if you'd ever figure it out,' he says.

He lifts up the blankets, as if he was opening the entrance to a cave, and says, 'Get in.'

Fact:
(Lucrezia Borgia's hair, curled like a snail, is pressed between glass in a reliquary at the Pinacoteca Ambrosiana, in Milan.)

Her hair is wheat-hair to be eaten, desert-coloured to be cocooned inside, straw-hair that suffocates and leaves an elbow, ribbon of thigh, light moon moments of skin exposed out of the tangled thicket.

Some touch, with little gentleness, try to knead themselves into her, into her twines and rope that gust with mildewed breath of bread, that in its chambers, nets of matted, knotted skeins are hidden poisons, and shells.

Within her threads some unbraid, unlace her lace, wonder at this yellow river whose yellow candle flame, one hundred coils, flower where they brush their lips.

In her black, stone-black, fairytale-black tower, she watches the white sails of sailboats move, and lilt and sway and swing, like empty wedding dresses.

12.

Emily is Not Submissive. This is a 'Terrifying Love'.
See: *Terrifying Love* by Walker, Lenore E.

The patron saint of lovers is Saint Valentine. The legend that surrounds this saint states that at the exact moment of his death, swallows, hawks and all birds chose their mates.

As Emily and Santi lie together in a room that had been Emily's mother's sewing room, Santi says, 'You can love your first cousin. It is not like loving a beast from the forest.'

Emily thinks he smells like melons, avocado leaves and pencils. In the dark Emily looks around the room and observes the shapes and shadows of her mother's things that look distorted in the night. She thinks her mother's sewing machine looks like an armadillo and that the hats that are lined up on one wall look like a row of birds standing on a wire. A small wicker basket in one corner looks like a rabbit.

Santiago says that he'd been watching her for weeks and had followed her to the orphanage and to the university. He broke into the house and lived there without any one noticing his presence. He watched Emily bathe, and listened to her telephone conversations. When she was not at home he sat in her room and smelled her clothes and perfumes and looked at her belongings.

'Some nights I just watched you sleep for hours until I fell asleep on the floor at the end of your bed,' Santi says. 'I'd creep out in the morning and hide someplace in the house.'

Santi calls her 'Cousin Emily'.

He sucks her hair. He kisses her hands. He licks his fingers and, using his saliva like ink, he draws pictures on her back. He draws volcanoes, a beehive, rain falling from clouds, and a serpent that twists and slides from the small of Emily's back up to her shoulders.

Santi says, 'Nothing has been hidden from me. I was your protector in a way. I have watched you brush your hair, file your nails, and cover your arms and neck with cream. I've listened to you urinate and cry.'

'When did I cry?' Emily asks. 'I never cry . . .'

'You cried on the day 'The Japanese' arrived at the orphanage. I wanted to lick the tears from your face. I wanted to hold you. During the night I cleaned away the tissues by your bed, but the next morning you didn't even notice,' Santi explains. He speaks quickly and breathlessly, as if he were running.

'No, I didn't notice,' Emily answers. 'Mother Agata says that I am still a child and naïve. I think she's right. You're not a book or a story. You are not a drawing on a page. And why would you hide and watch us?'

'I wanted to see if I liked you and your father. I wanted to see if I'd be welcome. My parents never talked about you, or this house, or anything, which, if you think about it, was strange and made me wonder.'

'Did you think we'd be monsters?'

'Well, maybe. It was easier for me to watch you than to knock on the front door.'

'Santi, we can never tell this to my father. He would not like this at all. I know him. He'd think you were dishonest.'

'There were so many things you never noticed. So I began to leave you my small presents. They were warnings for you,' Santi says as he strokes Emily's face with one finger. He draws over the outlines of her features, touches her eyebrows, the curve of her cheek, the bend of her chin. 'I liked to watch you react to them. They really frightened you, didn't they?'

'Yes,' Emily answers. 'I thought there was a thief in the house.' She remembers the fright she'd felt when she found the objects and the uneasiness of perceiving a scent of melons in her room that had lasted for days.

'I followed you everywhere. If I could have, I would have looked inside you – inside to your kidneys, spleen, heart and lungs . . .'

'I can't understand why anyone would do this. It makes me feel strange,' Emily says, cupping her hands over her eyes. 'You stalked me like a deer.'

'That's not true. I had not . . . I didn't know about you. I wanted to watch first and see if I wanted to claim my family. It was a way to be cautious. I am full of memories of what used to be. I felt a lack of hope and then I saw you open the front door and walk out of the house. I watched you pick up a jacaranda flower from the pavement and squeeze it into the palm of your hand. I thought you were just a bird that couldn't fly.'

'If I'm a bird, what are you?'

'I don't know how to be humble. Everything is my enemy. I am fighting everyone. My hands are always in fists. I never had a friend or an enemy. I was alone on that ranch always wondering when it was going to rain, smelling the air and listening for thunder. I have no treasures.'

'I also sleep with my hands clenched into fists. I've done it ever since I was a child. Sometimes Mother Agata had to pry them open.'

Emily takes Santi's hand and locks her fingers into his. 'I feel like everything in me is far away. My heart is far away from my hand. My hand is far away from my heart,' Emily whispers.

They lie still and quiet for a few minutes. Emily looks up at the ceiling and thinks the small shade that covers the light bulb looks like an owl.

Santi pushes the blankets down around Emily's waist and moves his palm over her stomach. He places his index finger inside her navel. He asks, 'Why are you so quiet? What are you thinking?'

'Nothing,' Emily whispers and kisses his mouth, which is the only feature on his face exactly like hers.

Emily is quiet because she hears voices in her mind. She hears what she knows people will say about her.

The lady from the vegetable store on the corner down from the house: *She was a good, a very good girl, although maybe a bit too spoiled by her father. And then her mother died so young. That could be it. You can't grow a tree in the shade. You can't get water from a stone. The splinter is like the tree.*

The priest: *She was raised like a nun. Honestly, a girl like that should be running around having some fun. It was a convent life. Maybe she should have become a nun. It would have kept her out of trouble, and that's for sure. May the Lord bless her and pardon her ways. Amen, I say.*

The neighbour's servant: *She had always worked at her grandmother's orphanage. Then she ran away with her cousin. I saw him a few times coming and going. He was very handsome, like an actor in the movies, but not like Pedro Infante, not that great. If he'd been my cousin, I would have run away with him too. Many people marry their cousins, but they just don't talk about it.*

Her fellow students at the university: *She felt shame. She could not face the world. She didn't even finish her studies and she was a good student, one of the best, really.*

Mother Agata: *I am sure she was a virgin completely inexperienced. Santi wrapped her in his arms, which were wings.*

Her father: *Someone said they went to Chihuahua. To think I welcomed him into my home . . .*

'God, I'm thirsty,' Santi says.

'Hush, hush,' Emily answers. 'Be careful, my father will hear us.'

'Don't worry, he's fast asleep by now,' Santi says in a whisper.

'So, what was it like on the ranch?' Emily asks. 'Tell me more about that. It was just you and your mother and father? You had no friends?'

'Yes. It was just the three of us, and a lot of dust. Just thinking about that place makes me thirsty. My parents were so in love with one another that it was as if I wasn't there. My father was even jealous of me. He was that way. A little wild but kind to the bone. But wild. I saw him kill a dog once that had bit my mother. He kicked the animal to death.'

'Santi, that's terrible. I'm shocked. I can't imagine that you are describing my father's brother! They sound so different.'

'From what I understand, there was no love lost between them. Yes, they're very different. Your father is civilised. I feel like I should be calling him "sir".'

'Do you want me to go and get a glass of water for you? I can slip down to the kitchen . . .'

'No,' Santi answers as he takes Emily's face in his hands. 'Let me taste your saliva.'

'What do I taste like?' Emily asks.

Fact:

Judith Ann Neeley met Mr Alvin Howard Neeley when she was

*fifteen years old. She thought, 'This is a man who takes whatever
he wants and he wants me.'*

*They drifted through Alabama, Florida, Louisiana and Texas
looking for rainbows and pots of gold.*

He called himself 'The Nightrider'.

She called herself 'Lady Sundance'.

*He'd say, 'Lady Sundance, let me tell you, nothing in this world
is ever going to get used up so that you can't have any. For you, this
is the land of plenty.'*

She'd say, 'You're just sugar to me.'

*He'd say, 'Lady Sundance, I'd buy you the moon if it was for sale.
Honest, I would. I can carry you. You are light as a feather, light
as a drop of rain, light as a little flower. I think you're a guitar or
violin maybe — just all hollow inside.'*

She'd say, 'But I make no music.'

*He'd say, 'I hear your love songs even if you don't sing any. You're
a song, baby, a beautiful song.'*

*They knew how to pull out a gun from under their coats and
jackets and march people through the trees.*

*They collected souvenirs from their victims and even kept photo-
graphs they found in people's wallets: a girl in a birthday party hat;
a bride and a groom and a wedding cake; a man in a boat; a child
taking a bath with three rubber ducks; and three women smiling
and holding a bottle of champagne in the air.*

*One photograph is of a yellow and white canary in a birdcage
hanging from a long hook on a porch. Its tiny, black bead-eyes look
straight into the camera. This is Judith Ann's favourite photograph.*

She'd say, 'What stupid motherfucker carries a picture of a canary in his wallet?'

Lady Sundance knows all the parts of a smoothbore shotgun by heart:

Butt plate
Stock
Pistol grip
Trigger guard
Trigger
Hammer
Breechblock
Forearm
Barrel
Ventilated rib
Muzzle
Front sight.

He'd say, 'Remember the first time, you were shy like a young doe, wanting to talk to these people and make them feel like it was a picnic in the woods, like it was some kind of party or something. You'd ask about the weather, or you'd ask them their names, or where they were from, like we were going to have a conversation or something. Like you were carrying sandwiches in your bag.'

She'd say, 'I had to get used to this kind of loving. I didn't know loving and killing was a way to be.'

13.

The Day Hipolito is Stung by a Scorpion

Emily wakes up at six in the morning, quietly slips out of Santi's bed, and goes to her room. She puts on a bathrobe and bathes and brushes her teeth and combs her hair and puts on her earrings and a dress and shoes and picks up her bag and puts it back down and goes back to the bathroom and paints on some lipstick and combs her hair and touches her cheek and touches her heart and combs her hair again and brushes her teeth again and goes back into her bedroom and touches her cheek and touches her cheek and touches her cheek and touches her mouth and and and and

As Emily walks from her house to the orphanage she thinks that on this day the city is *Mexico Tenochtitlan*, ancient and quiet. Several street sweepers are out and clean the ground with their long, witch-like brooms made from tree branches.

Across the street a servant dressed in a chequered pink

and white dress and a white apron walks a black Labrador puppy on a leash.

A group of adolescents in navy blue government school uniforms, who are obviously skipping school, lean against green and pink walls smoking cigarettes. The girls have folded over the waists on their skirts in order to turn them into miniskirts. They have also pushed their knee-high blue socks down to their ankles. Their lips are covered with brown lipstick. One boy and a girl kiss passionately. Emily can see their tongues as they rock in and away from each other.

The streets, pavement and walls are made of stone. As Emily walks she observes stone gargoyles of dog-like figures, stone virgins and stone crosses and figures of Christ that are in wall niches, above doors or placed to the side of doorways. Framed by all this stone, the jacaranda trees fill the air with a violet light. The bougainvillea flowers are pink and red and look soft and dull in the early morning.

Emily takes a deep breath. She can smell the stone and sun and dust. She remembers a passage from one of the books that her great-grandfather had in his library and that she has read dozens of times over the years. The book is called *Encyclopaedia of Mother's Advice*, and was published in Chicago, USA, in 1905 and, Emily thinks, was probably bought in Mexico instead of being shipped over from Britain. In the book there is a chapter on courage. Emily remembers it by heart: *One may possess physical courage, so that*

in times of danger, a railroad accident, a steamboat collision or a
runaway horse, the heart will not be daunted or the cheek paled,
while on the other hand, one may be morally brave, not afraid to
speak a word for the right in season, though unwelcome, to perform
a disagreeable duty unflinchingly or to refuse to do a wrong act,
and yet be a physical coward, trembling and terrified in a thunder-
storm, timid in the dark, and even scream at the sight of a mouse.

The book has always fascinated Emily since *Mother's Advice* is something that she has never had. She read the book hoping to find tips and womanly secrets. The book has chapters called 'The Art of Beauty In Dress'; 'All About Kitchen Work and Invalid Cookery'; and 'How To Be Handsome'. But there is no chapter on love.

Emily feels she is in a railroad accident, a steamboat collision and on a runaway horse. She can sense the presence of a thunderstorm.

At the orphanage everyone is in an uproar because a scorpion has stung Hipolito. He had been sitting on a bench in the patio reading a book when he leaned over to pick up his glass of orange water and placed his hand, palm down, right on top of the insect.

Mother Agata killed the scorpion with a broom and placed it in a jar for all the children to see.

'At least it's a brown one,' Mother Agata says to Emily. 'It is not like those dangerous ones from the state of Durango. Those white transparent ones can kill you in a few minutes.'

'Did he have any reaction to the sting?' Emily asks.

'He's fine. Of course, it was a shock but now I think he feels rather proud of it all happening to him.'

The children are horrified. They pick up the jar and shake it to see if the scorpion will come back to life. They examine its large front pincers and venomous tail.

Emily tells the children about the people in the city of Durango who spend their lives hunting the insects to earn a living. At one time there were so many that the state government paid its residents for any scorpion, dead or alive, that was brought into the government headquarters. Some people in Durango claim that in 1784 the city bought 600,000 scorpions.

Emily explains to the children that there are many species of scorpions: common striped scorpion, brown scorpion, giant hairy scorpion, devil scorpion and sculptured scorpion. 'Even their names are scary, don't you think?' Emily adds.

Hipolito shows his hand to everyone, but there is nothing to see. He feels the poison's burn, but his hand looks the same. There is not the slightest trace of where the sharp tail entered his skin.

'Sometimes you don't know what has hurt you if you don't find the beast,' Mother Agata explains. 'Many people get stung and they don't even know what happened to them. They just feel a sharp pain. Some people have terrible allergic reactions and have to be taken to a hospital.'

Mother Agata tells the children that the scorpion belongs to Hipolito since he was the one stung by it.

Hipolito holds the jar with the scorpion close to his chest, as if it was an amulet. He says that he wants to take the scorpion up to Angelica's room and show it to her and marches proudly toward her room.

Emily follows behind him. 'I'm coming with you, Hipolito,' she says. 'Wait for me.'

Angelica is lying on her bed and reading in the dark. Her head is pressed close to the book. She is covered by one weightless, white cotton sheet. The curtains are drawn. No one understands how she sees to read the letters on the page.

'I don't want to see the scorpion,' Angelica says and presses her face into the book. 'Go away.'

'I am sorry,' Hipolito says. 'I thought you'd like to see it. It stung me when I was reading downstairs on the bench.'

'No! No! No!' Angelica says emphatically. 'Get it out of my room. I don't want that jar in here!'

'Hipolito is only trying to be nice,' Emily says. 'He just wants to show you what hurt him. Try not to be angry, he means well.'

'I don't care!' Angelica shrieks as she hides her head under the cotton sheet. 'I cannot look at that horrible thing. Get out!'

'It is so ugly. It looks like a monster. Look at it, please,' Hipolito begs.

Angelica suddenly sits straight up on her bed and throws the sheet off her body. The fabric flies off her shoulders like a wing. Emily and Hipolito take a step backward when they see that she is completely naked. Hipolito takes in a large gulp of air. The scarring across Angelica's chest looks like mother of pearl, as if her body were the inside of an oyster shell. 'Leave me now,' she whispers severely.

Fact:

moor, noun. A tract of unenclosed waste ground; now usually uncultivated ground covered with heather; a heath.

(OED)

In one of Myra Hindley's letters she described her love for Ian Brady. She said that she could not resist him and used this as an excuse to justify her role in the murders. She wrote that he had 'such a powerful personality, such an overwhelming charisma. If he'd told me the moon was made of green cheese or that the sun rose in the west I would have believed him.'

On Saddleworth Moor the diggers did not find grooved ware pottery, bluestones, bone daggers, iron shards, bone points, Celtic bronze jugs, urn fields, runes or Roman coins. It was a landscape of shale banks, peat, turf, gully and grass.

On Saddleworth Moor the sun rises in the west.

14.

Marriage in a World of Rattlesnakes, Wolves and Mammoth Bones

As Emily enters the front door of her house the hallway is dark and only a lean shaft of light from the living room indicates that someone is home. As she takes two steps inside she can hear her father's music. He is listening to a song by Agustin Lara on the old 1950s record player. Lara spent most of his life playing the piano in brothels. The woman he loved was killed in the brothel when she put herself between Lara's body and a pistol that was shot at him by a military officer. This man was jealous of Lara's love for this woman. Everybody in Mexico knows this. Emily knows that Lara was very ugly, but women adored him. He had even married Maria Felix.

Emily's father listens to the song called 'Woman'.

> *Woman, divine woman,*
> *you have the poison that fascinates in your eyes,*

woman you have the perfume
of an orange tree in bloom.

Emily enters the room and sits down beside her father. She leans toward him and he kisses her cheek. He explains that Santi is not there because he had to go out for a job interview. 'He left early, right after you left for the orphanage and he hasn't been back since. It does seem rather late.'

'I'm sure he'll be back shortly,' Emily answers. 'Shall I get us something to eat?'

As Emily walks to the kitchen she thinks that even though Santi has only been in their house for a few days he has turned their quiet world upside down. She realises that when Santi was not there she and her father were on edge, listening for his arrival. And when he was home his music, footsteps, his smell, voice and laughter filled every room.

Emily opens the refrigerator and removes a few green tomatoes, an onion, a small green hot pepper and a handful of fresh coriander. She opens a kitchen drawer and takes out a small paring knife and chops the ingredients together with some garlic and a teaspoon of salt.

As she cooks she notices that Santi's beer bottles have been left in the sink. One of his sweaters is draped over a kitchen chair. She also notices that a pair of his shoes, with his socks stuffed into them, has been left under the kitchen table.

She warms some flour tortillas filled with cheese. She hears her father stand up and walk over to the record player and play the same song over again. Emily places the light supper on a tray and carries it into the living room.

'Would you like something to drink?' Emily asks as she walks toward the liquor cabinet and takes out a bottle of tequila and two shot glasses. 'It's been a long day.'

'Yes, I'll have some,' her father answers. 'Today I was looking at some early family photographs and I realised that nobody ever smiled. Smiling is a modern thing.'

'You're right. No one smiles. It wasn't the custom.'

'It's quite refreshing, if you ask me.'

'I knew you'd say that,' Emily answers. 'I promise never to smile in a photograph again.'

Emily and her father sit quietly for a few minutes. They listen to the whistle of the man who sells bread as he passes by the window on his bicycle.

Emily tells her father the story about Hipolito being stung by a scorpion that very morning at the orphanage.

'Even these have practically disappeared,' Emily's father answers. 'I remember, as a child, I used to find them all the time. They travel in pairs. You knew that if you killed one, you'd find another nearby. It gave you an uneasy feeling. Mostly they appeared near the kitchen sink or among the towels and bedclothes. We always checked our beds and shoes. Nobody thinks about doing this any more.'

'Mother Agata killed it and put in a glass jar for everyone to examine,' Emily says. 'Angelica would not even look at it.'

'Of course,' Emily's father answers. 'She is lost inside herself. It's understandable. Poor darling.'

'Mother Agata says she found Angelica sucking on small stones from the gravel path in the garden. When Mother Agata told her not to, Angelica said that the stones were deliciously cold, like ice.'

Emily's father rubs his eyes. 'Over the years,' he says, 'there have been so many orphans who have come and gone. Each one has had their story and secrets. Some are almost too much to bear. I remember one of the saddest cases of all. I was a boy back then. There was a little girl called Andrea who could never accept that her parents had died. You've heard about her, haven't you?' Emily's father asks.

'Yes,' Emily answers. 'You've told me. That little girl used to run away all the time, didn't she? She was always looking for her parents.'

'Your grandmother had to tie her to her bed at night so that she wouldn't escape. Eventually she did escape. She actually gnawed through the pink ballet-shoe ribbons that she was tied with. Your grandmother probably tied her with perfect pretty bows! Can you imagine, ballet-shoe ribbons? That's the part I never forget! Andrea never came back and we never heard from her again. She was only eleven years old when she disappeared.'

'Where did she come from?'

'I'm not too sure. I vaguely remember that a policeman who brought her to the orphanage found her in the street. The little girl was furious and kicking and screaming. The only thing she liked to do was to take baths. The policeman said that she'd been found sleeping in a doorway. She had a strange guitar with her that was made from the body of an armadillo. That instrument is probably around somewhere in the orphanage.'

'Mother Agata is worried that Angelica will get sick from the cold things she finds to put into her mouth,' Emily answers.

Emily and her father sit silently for a few minutes. After a while Emily's father gets up and pours some more tequila into his glass and serves himself another tortilla with cheese and green tomato sauce. 'So,' he asks. 'What do you think of Santiago?'

'I don't know . . .' Emily says. 'One question, though, before I go to bed. Were you and your brother Charles very different?'

'We were different as any two brothers are, but not fundamentally different. Why do you ask?'

'It's nothing really. It's just that when Santi has described him he seems so completely different to you. He sounds very Mexican. Santi says he never spoke in English.'

'It's probably just Santi's point of view.'

'Perhaps you're right,' Emily answers. She picks up her empty plate and places it down on the tray.

'By the way, do you know what I saw today?' Emily's father asks as he sits up in his chair and rubs his neck.

'No, tell me.'

'I saw two small lizards in the garden. It has been a long time since I've seen a lizard there.'

'When I was a child, the garden was full of lizards.'

'Yes, it's true.'

'I remember that Roberto, our servant Concha's little boy, would grab them by the jaw, between his forefinger and thumb, and this would make them go into some kind of trance . . .'

'Yes, they play dead.'

'Then he would clip them on our earlobes like earrings and when we pulled them off they would scurry away.'

'You never told me about that.'

'Concha told us that the lizards could crawl inside our ears and make us go crazy, so we stopped.'

'It'll be interesting to see if the lizards are still there tomorrow. I hope a bird doesn't get them.'

'They'll still be there, I'm sure,' Emily says and lightly kisses her father's cheek. 'Goodnight. I'll see you in the morning.'

As Emily walks to her room, she passes by Santi's bedroom. The door is open. She can see that his shoes and two pairs of cowboy boots stand in a row and his books are stacked in piles on the table and on the floor against the wall.

Emily walks into the room and looks around more carefully. His accordion rests on a chair. In one corner she can see his architectural drawings, which are rolled up and held together with red rubber bands.

From here Emily can still hear her father's music as it rises up into the second floor of the house:

> *Woman, divine woman,*
> *you have the poison that fascinates in your eyes,*
> *woman you have the perfume*
> *of an orange tree in bloom.*

As Emily turns to leave the room she sees a black and white framed photograph propped up against a lamp on the old sewing machine. The photograph is of Santi's parents: his mother is sitting outside on a bench that must have been the ranch's front porch. Her black hair is braided in a long coil that falls over her left shoulder. Santi's father stands behind her with his hands on her head as if he were blessing her. She is wearing a simple white dress and holds three white roses in her hand. Her face is unrecognisable since it is darkened and completely erased by Santi's father's shadow. Emily cannot make out the features. In the dark she looks like a piece of obsidian, the beginning of the world, Eve.

Emily realises that it must be Santi's parents' wedding photograph. They are not smiling. It is marriage in a world of rattlesnakes, wolves and mammoth bones.

Fact:

'It is as if a great big black bird is following me everywhere,' she'd say. 'It is if I were constantly followed by its black shadow. I think there is a dark wing above me.'

She never left her house in search of death. Death was as close to her as the washing machine, ironing board and television set. Death was down the hall, though a door and in a crib. Death was under a hand-knitted blanket made with pink or blue wool.

There are nomadic killers, territorial killers and stationary killers. Marybeth Tinning was a stationary killer.

Munchausen's Syndrome by Proxy is a mental illness named after Baron Von Munchausen (1720–97), who was a German soldier who told exaggerated stories about his campaigning adventures. This illness describes a compulsive need for sympathy, which leads patients to claim false illnesses and tragedies. In some cases the psychosis is so severe that patients will inflict self-injuries and even kill their own children for sympathy.

Marybeth Tinning liked people to hold her, bring her flowers and call on her to see how she was doing. She especially liked it when people brought her tuna fish casseroles and apple pies.

'Oh, you shouldn't have. Really, you shouldn't have,' she would say. 'How kind.'

Marybeth Tinning liked to wear black clothes, mourning clothes. She liked to go to funeral parlours and pick out the nicest coffin she could find. She favoured the ones lined with white satin since these had a small pillow for a child's head sewn into the lining and, she thought, looked like beds.

114

Marybeth Tinning liked funerals and would spend days preparing for them. She'd go to the beauty parlour and have her hair dyed and coiffed and she'd have her nails painted. She always bought a new dress and it was always black. Sometimes she didn't wear gloves so that everyone could admire her pretty pink nail polish.

'You have to get spruced up for death,' she'd say. 'I have to look pretty for heaven and my baby. I have to smell good for heaven and my baby.'

Her husband, Joseph Tinning, said, 'You have to trust your wife. She has her things to do, and as long as she gets them done, you don't ask questions.'

From 1972 to 1985, Marybeth Tinning lost nine of her children.

Her husband, Joseph Tinning, said, 'You have to trust your wife. She has her things to do, and as long as she gets them done, you don't ask questions.'

Marybeth Tinning never cried. When people asked her how she could live without weeping all the time, she'd say, 'I can't mess up my make-up. That would be a real shame. I cry inside. The tears go backward inside of me and nobody can see them. But they hurt anyway. They're really dripping inside of me like an open faucet.'

After the trial everyone remembered that Marybeth Tinning had lost nine children and had never shed a tear. 'Not even one crocodile tear for show,' someone said. 'Not even nine tears.'

After the trial everyone said that Tinning had a classic case of 'Munchausen's Syndrome by Proxy'.

After the trial her husband, Joseph Tinning, said, 'You have to trust your wife. She has her things to do, and as long as she gets them done, you don't ask questions.'

15.

'In loving memory of Emily, the beloved wife of Thomas J. Edwards, who died at Pachuca May 3rd, 1897, aged 30 years.'

Emily lies in bed in the dark. She cannot fall asleep. Every car that drives past in the street lights up her room. She can hear her father's slow, thought-out footsteps as he goes up to his bedroom and closes the door. She lies very still, stretched out on her back with her hands folded on her stomach. Emily listens for another sound, for the new footsteps, new voice, the new hands in her hands.

At midnight she lies on her left side and thinks about the orphan, Andrea, who had a guitar made from an armadillo shell. She thinks about musical instruments that have been made from animals – flutes out of bones, drums out of hides. She thinks that she is an instrument with her heart beating like an ancient drum.

At twelve-thirty she lies on her right side. She suddenly thinks that she can smell melons and grapes. Emily rubs her eyes and remembers the time that her father took her to visit the British Cemetery in Real del Monte, where the Cornish miners had been buried. She had been twelve years old at the time.

The graveyard lay at the top of a steep hill, which meant that they could see down to the valley and the chain of mountains that form the Sierra Madre stretching out before them. They'd arrived early in the morning and the gate was locked. A vicious-looking dog was inside, guarding the land. Emily and her father stood outside staring at the ancient wall and wrought iron gate. An hour later the watchman appeared with the key attached to a rope that was wrapped around his tattered and dusty clothes.

Emily and her father spent an hour in the chilly mountain air walking among the graves and reading the gravestones. The most beautiful graves, with stone angels on them, belonged to the John Rule family. John Rule was appointed commissioner of the mines in 1858.

'Have you found your grave?' her father had asked with a laugh.

'What do you mean?' she'd answered, confused by his question.

'You've already been buried here,' he'd said. 'Why do you think you were named Emily?'

He took her hand and led her to the back wall. Emily stood staring at the tomb that was covered with lichen, which had turned it a dark green. The carved words in the stone had been difficult to read. Her father had read them aloud to her, 'In loving memory of Emily, the beloved wife of Thomas J. Edwards, who died at Pachuca May 3rd, 1897, aged 30 years.'

'But she wasn't a relative, right? You're kidding,' she'd said.

'Of course, darling,' he'd said. 'I'm kidding you.'

'She was so young. I wonder who she was.'

'A British miner's wife and only that,' he'd answered.

At one o'clock Emily sits up in bed. She can hear the high-pitched sound of the night watchman's whistle as he walks around the neighbourhood. Emily remembers when 'The Japanese' arrived at the orphanage with their clothes cut up in pieces to fit around their plaster casts and bandages. She remembers that that was the day she found her pillow thrown on the floor and her bedding opened as if someone had been sleeping in her bed. Now she knew that Santi had used her room, touched her things, and, yes, he had slept in her bed.

At two she listens to the sound of a police car's siren as it drives past. Emily recalls the stories about Lizzie MacDonald, the very first child to live at the orphanage. She'd been the daughter of a Scottish miner. Emily's father told her that since Lizzie had been all alone in that enormous building Emily's great-grandmother had bought the child a parrot. The story that had been passed down was that the little Scottish girl had taught the bird to speak words in English and to say 'Lizzie'. Apparently, the bird cried out the girl's name until it died many years after Lizzie had gone back to Scotland.

Emily thinks about Santi's telegram, the red apple on her bed, and the arrowhead.

At two-thirty a.m. she finally hears the sound of the front door lock open and Santi's footsteps enter the house. She listens to him walk into the sewing room and, after a short while, he steps into Emily's bedroom and quietly undresses at the foot of her bed.

'I'm here,' he whispers as he lifts up the wool blankets and gets into bed beside her. 'I've just arrived this minute. Are you awake?'

'Where have you been?' Emily asks. 'Of course I'm awake. I was beginning to worry.'

'I met up with some architects I used to know. We went to university together. We went to a canteen for a drink or two,' Santi answers. 'I didn't realise that it was so late.'

She can smell cigars, cigarettes and pulque, the bitter smell of fermented cactus, on his skin and hair.

'Are you drunk?' She asks.

'Just a little, just a little bit,' he answers and laughs softly. 'There was this great pianist there who played Frank Sinatra's songs. You would have loved it. He must have played "As Times Goes By" a dozen times.'

Emily does not answer.

'You're so quiet. Are you going to punish me?' Santi asks.

'I thought that maybe you were not coming back,' Emily

says. 'I thought you'd left. I thought I'd never see you again.'

'Those are just silly night fears. In Chihuahua when someone is frightened at night we say that the spirit of the owl is inside of them,' Santi says as he strokes Emily's hair away from her face. 'I think an owl has been here.'

'I couldn't help myself, I thought you'd disappeared,' Emily whispers. 'Because of what happened, I thought maybe . . .'

'I would never disappear,' Santiago answers and takes her face in his hands and kisses her forehead. 'You sound like a little girl and not the perfectly tamed, perfectly controlled woman that I know.'

'Do you think I'm so tame?' Emily asks.

'Oh, yes, you do everything that's expected of you. You're good and responsible, so well brought up. You do nothing surprising. Even when you were alone and I watched you, you never did anything that wasn't perfect, even prissy,' Santi answers.

'Then why do you want to be with me if I am so boring?' Emily asks as she sits up in bed and leans away from him. She closes her eyes and crosses her arms in front of her.

'Are you angry?' Santi asks. 'Please don't be angry with me. I'm sorry.'

'Well, if that is what you think . . .'

'I didn't mean to hurt your feelings,' Santi interrupts. 'I guess I just can't believe it when I meet someone who is so controlled by society's rules and expectations. You know all about facts. You know all about other people's lives and even the lives of saints. But what about your life, Emily?' he asks. 'I wonder, have you ever done anything unexpected?'

'I don't know, Santi,' Emily answers. 'I have never thought about it before.'

'Have you hit anyone?' Santi asks.

'No.'

'Have you broken anything on purpose?' Santi asks.

'No.'

'Actually, that's not true,' Santi says. 'How strange. Don't you remember?'

'What are you talking about?' Emily asks.

'One day when I was watching you, I saw you sit right here on your bed. It was late at night. I could watch you from a crack in the door. I saw you take a dress out of the closet and tear it to pieces. I watched you rip it with your hands.'

Emily leans back on her elbows. 'Oh, yes, I do. I remember,' Emily says. 'But it was worn out. I tore it up to use the pieces as rags, kitchen rags. I do this with some of my old clothes.'

'I don't believe you,' Santi says. 'You did it so violently. I loved seeing that side of you.'

'I don't lie,' Emily answers. 'Do you?'

'Of course I do. Everyone does. Except I don't lie for

important things. So, I am not lying when I say that I won't leave you, that I won't disappear.'

Emily leans back on the pillow. She turns away from Santi. She thinks: *Disappeared. An eleven-letter word. Disappeared like a lost ring, a sweater, and a spoon. Vanished. This is a word with eight letters. Vanished like early morning fog and dew. Vanished into the magician's hat. Lost is a four-letter word. Lost into a genie's lamp. Missing is a seven-letter word.*

Emily thinks: *One morning she woke up, she bathed and dressed, she left her bag on the sofa, placed one hundred pesos in her pocket, turned on the water pump and went to the market to buy some fruit. She did not leave a note.*

The police investigation, which included interviewing people at the Coyoacan market, states that Emily's mother bought four apples, a papaya, a dozen lemons and a kilo of guayabas. At another stall she bought some black thread.

The police report states:

Married name: Neale
Paternal name: Kilronan
Proper name: Margaret
Nationality: Irish
Skin: white
Hair: black
Eyes: blue
Height: 1.60 mts.
Weight: 55 kilos.

Day of disappearance: 16 May 1978

Last sighting: the Coyoacan market. 11 a.m.

Last seen wearing: long black cotton skirt, white blouse, brown, flat shoes.

Like the butterflies and beetles, like the pepper trees and telegrams, Emily's mother disappeared.

Emily knows that she vanished on 16 May, the feast day of John Nepomucene. He is the patron saint of silence and bridges.

Santiago quickly falls asleep – the deep, uncomfortable sleep of someone who has had too much to drink. While he rests Emily stares across the dark room and out the open window and listens to him breathe. She thinks: *Lost is a four-letter word. Lost into a genie's lamp. Missing is a seven-letter word.* She counts the letters on her fingers.

Emily keeps her eyes open in the dark and thinks about the first time she saw Santi, when he was in the library looking at her father's butterfly collection. His voice fills her mind and she can hear him saying, 'That railway track was like a long river. Everyone followed it, everything happened on it. There was always some container that leaked so the train tracks would get sprinkled with grains of sugar. Then a few dozen desert mice and rabbits would appear out of nowhere to lick the sugar off the ties.' She also hears him say, 'I saw my father kill a dog once that had bit my mother. He kicked the animal to death.'

At six in the morning, when the long strokes of the street sweeper's broom can be heard outside, she gently strokes Santi's arm and wakes him.

'You'd better go back to your room now,' Emily says. 'It's morning. Wake up.'

Santi stretches and murmurs, 'Five more minutes.'

'No,' Emily answers. 'My father will be waking up soon.'

'I don't care,' he answers as he covers his face with his hands. 'You pull me farther and farther towards you,' he says. 'I want you.'

'Please,' Emily insists.

'He'll have to know eventually,' Santiago says as he gets up and stretches his arms in the air.

'Maybe. But not yet.'

Santi leans over and kisses Emily's forehead. He sweeps his fingers through her hair. 'As I was waking up I was thinking that all words have a sex. Words are male or female. I was thinking about this just now. The sea is a woman, but the ocean is a man. A chair is a girl.'

'Was this a dream?' Emily asks.

'No. No. I woke up thinking about this.'

'Well, it's true in Spanish, but in English words are not male or female.'

'Yes, of course they are. You just feel it innately, that's the difference.'

'So is a mirror a man or a woman?'

'That's a difficult question and my head hurts,' Santi

says and yawns. 'I think I had too much to drink last night.'

'Do you drink a lot?' Emily asks.

'Not a lot, but I do like to drink.' He gets out of bed and picks up his clothes that are in a pile on the floor.

Outside they hear the soft whistle of the man who sells bread.

'Can you do me a favour?' Santi asks.

'Yes, what is it?'

'Do you mind not wearing that cross?' Santi asks, pointing at her neck with his index finger.

Emily touches the small, gold cross that hangs from a chain around her neck. 'It belonged to my mother,' Emily answers. 'I don't understand. I've always worn it. Why?'

'I don't like it. I don't like religious symbols.'

'This is ridiculous,' Emily answers. 'You don't want me to wear this? Why?'

'It's the first thing that I've asked you to do and you say no to me,' Santi says turning away from her.

'But why?' Emily says. She gets out of bed and walks toward Santi. 'Why?' she repeats again.

'Do as you wish,' he says. 'But think of this, Cousin Emily,' he adds as he walks out the door. 'You've refused to do the first thing asked of you. It tells me a lot. What kind of love is this?'

Emily watches her bedroom door close behind Santi and sits on the end of her bed. She holds the small, gold cross in her right hand and stares out of the window. She feels her heart beat in her hands. After a few minutes she hears the sound of music coming from Santi's room. She recognises that it is Jimi Hendrix again:

> *Well, I'm standing here freezing*
> *inside your golden garden*
> *got my ladder*
> *leaned up against your wall . . .*

Fact:
Silver pincers,
pins and needles,
branding irons,
red-hot pokers,
whips,
and scissors.
   Silence.
   Erzsebet Báthory was born in 1560 into the Polish Báthory clan under the Order of the Dragon. She killed from 300 to 650 women. They were mostly poor peasants who came to see her hoping to find work. Everyone who went to labour in her home disappeared.
   Some people in the village said they heard the sounds of wild animals when they walked past her house.
   Nobody ever thought that it was the wind.
   Some people said that the sound could be the noise of a caged bear. Other people thought it was the sound of a flock of crows. These sounds were imagined since there was only silence.

She was known as the 'Bloody Countess'.

Erzsebet was beautiful, with large black eyes that made her look child-like and frightened. She had soft, smooth skin like apple-skin, plum-skin, peach-skin, grape-skin, pear-skin.

Her old nurse, Ilona Joo, helped carry the dead victims to the forest, where they would be eaten by wolves.

Erzsebet wore five-strand ropes of pearls around her neck above large, square lace collars. She wore a ring on every finger, even on her thumbs. Everyone said she looked just like any mother's daughter. Everyone said she had good manners. She always said please and thank you and covered her mouth when she coughed.

There was only silence because she knew how to thread a needle. She knew how to sew and darn. Her needlework was exquisite. She could hem a dress in five minutes.

She sewed her victims' mouths closed.

She practised different kinds of stitches:

long and short stitch,

fishbone stitch,

chain stitch.

She had a large cage, like a birdcage, made by the ironmongers at a nearby village. They soldered large sharp spikes inside the cage.

It was a prison.

A birdcage without whistles or songs.

A large pincushion.

16.

What Happens When People Disappear

'How do you fall off the edge of the world?' Emily thinks to herself. Someone must have said this to her as a child and the sentence remained inside her like a song: *How do you fall off the edge of the world?*

Emily imagines her mother walking down an empty cobblestone street that is barren of houses, trees, and street lamps. It is the street of a child's drawing made with white chalk on the pavement. It is a street where a child only drew long-stemmed flowers as tall as trees and buildings. She imagines her mother walking in a perfectly straight line with her arms down at her sides until she falls at the edge of the horizon as if she'd fallen off a cliff.

When the children at the orphanage ask Emily what happened to her mother, and she tells them that she disappeared, they become distraught. They stare at her face. They don't know if she is telling the truth or just teasing them.

Emily's father never talks about what happened. It is only

through Mother Agata that Emily has an idea of what those days, weeks, months and years were like for her father. Mother Agata says that at first Emily's father lived in a panic. He couldn't sleep and would begin to tremble every time the telephone rang or someone came to the front door.

'I think he was both terrified that your mother would be found and terrified that she would not be found. This always happens when someone disappears,' Mother Agata explains.

Emily's father never got rid of her mother's belongings or changed anything in the house. The closets in his bedroom are still filled with her blouses and dresses. The shoe racks still hold her dusty shoes that for some reason Emily never dared to try on. She did not want to step in her mother's steps.

'Perhaps he really thought she'd come back,' Mother Agata says.

The drawers on the left-hand side of the bedroom dresser still contain her scarves, evening bags, hair clips, hairbrushes, jewellery, face creams, lipsticks and perfumes.

Nobody knows what happened.

'How does somebody fall off the edge of the world?' Emily asks.

At the time when people were questioned, everyone had a different story to tell.

One woman, who was buying fish at the market, said she thought she saw Emily's mother get into a taxi. The woman said that two or three other people were with her. She noticed that they were carrying umbrellas even though it was the dry season.

The man who sold her the lemons said Emily's mother was with a tall Chinese man who was about fifty years old and looked like an actor from a Kung Fu movie.

The young girl who sold Emily's mother the black thread said she was crying and blowing her nose. When the young girl asked 'What's the matter?', Emily's mother had answered: 'I am turning into a piece of silver. The number 925 is branded on my arm. I'm leaving my daughter and I'm leaving my husband because they're better off without me. Nobody will ever forgive a mother who can abandon her child. I am a mermaid like the story of "The Little Mermaid". My legs are going to turn into a fishtail. I have to go to the sea or I'm going to die.'

The old woman, who had a film of white cataracts covering her black pupils and who sold Emily's mother the guava apples, said that her mother was carrying a baby in her arms wrapped in a heavy wool shawl with black and brown stripes on it, which looked like the kind of shawls that are woven outside Toluca.

The street sweeper said he saw her get into a police car. He said that she was screaming and kicking and that the police had trouble getting her into the car. The following day, when the police interrogated him for a second time, the street sweeper said that in actual fact he had seen her get on a bus. In order to try to get the story straight, Emily's father went to the market to speak to the man, but the street sweeper said that he'd never seen Emily's mother at all and to leave him alone.

When Emily was a child, Mother Agata used to comfort her by quoting Saint John of the Cross. 'A bird can be held by a chain or by a thread, still it cannot fly,' she'd say and stroke Emily's hair. She asked Emily to imagine that her mother was like a bird, flying free, a bird that flew even at night and never needed to rest.

The children at the orphanage echo each other over the years. They all think the same thing: if Emily's mother was lost, why didn't anyone look for her and find her? Like finding a lost shoe under the bed.

The orphans know that they cannot find their own parents. Once when 'The Japanese' couldn't find their favourite book about horses, Hipolito said to Emily with exasperation, 'Well, it's just like your mother! It's exactly like your mother! Completely lost! I can't find it anywhere!'

When Santi leaves her bedroom in the morning, Emily sits motionless for a few minutes. A pickup truck carrying an enormous load of oranges slowly drives past the house. From the back of the truck a man, who is dressed in blue jeans and a T-shirt that has 'The Sex Pistols' written across it, cries out through an orange plastic bullhorn, 'Oranges for you. The most beautiful oranges for you. The sweetest oranges for you.' For a few seconds Emily's room is drenched with the smell of ripe oranges. A few bees enter through her window and quickly leave to follow the swarm of bees that pursue the truck.

She can still hear his words in her mind: *It is the first thing I asked you to do and you've said no to me. Do as you wish. But think of this, Cousin Emily, you've refused to do the first thing I've asked of you. It tells me a lot.*

Emily unclips the chain and takes off the small gold cross and places it in a box on her dresser. She has not removed it for years. 'It was my mother's cross,' she thinks to herself as she touches the place on her chest, over her sternum, over her heart, where it rested against her skin. She thinks, 'It is a part of me, another piece of bone. The gold metal has always been warm, sometimes warmer than my own hands.'

After Emily's mother disappeared, her father tried to be both father and mother to Emily. He took her to ballet lessons on Francisco Sosa Street. He took her to buy her first toe shoes at the Miguelito ballet shop and accompanied her to the hairdresser to get her hair trimmed. When Emily liked to wear braids, he'd clumsily do his best. He made sure her clothes were clean and ironed. He read books to her and told her stories. He helped her sharpen her pencils.

Emily's father never missed a school play, dance performance or school fair. He always sat in the front row so that she could see him as he clapped over-enthusiastically. He clapped for two people and loved for two, listened for two and dreamed for two.

Emily inherited her father's inquisitiveness. While he researched the lives of insects that had disappeared from the valley of Mexico, she read all kinds of books.

Mother Agata says to Emily, 'It was always strange to go over to your house. It was very quiet there – just the sound of wings and pages. You were always looking at some book while your father counted his insects.'

Mother Agata explains that Emily loves maps and strange facts and books because it is a way of looking for her mother. 'You like to find conclusions.'

'Yes, it is true,' Emily answers. 'I like to know about endings, about what happened.'

'That's because your mother's life never ended. The door or window is never closed. Yes, that's right: you live in a house with an open window. As a child you used to ask me if someone was giving food and water to your mother. This is what happens when someone just disappears. Only Saint Anthony of Padua can help you.'

'Yes, yes, I know. The saint of lost articles, barren women, the poor, shipwrecks and travellers.'

'He is also invoked against starvation. You missed that one,' Mother Agata adds.

'That's strange,' Emily answers. 'I always feel hungry.'

When Emily arrives at the orphanage she goes straight to Mother Agata's office to see what lessons are scheduled for the day.

Mother Agata is sitting behind her desk reading the

newspaper. 'It's good to see you, Emily,' she says placing the newspaper to one side and standing up. 'For the past few days I've been feeling the earth tremble. You know I'm sensitive to trembling. There's going to be an earthquake for sure.'

'I promised the children I'd give them a class in amazing facts today,' Emily says as she walks toward the window and looks up at the sky. 'Do you really think there might be an earthquake?'

Mother Agata walks over to Emily and stands beside her, leans over at the waist because she is so tall, and encircles her with one arm. They both look at the sliver of a child's moon in the blue and grey Mexican sky. Emily can smell her cologne of lemon water.

'Earthquakes don't happen in the sky, why are you looking up? You should be looking at the ground,' Mother Agata says with a laugh.

'It's a beautiful moon,' Emily answers. 'It looks blue.'

'What facts are you going to teach the children then?' Mother Agata asks.

'I thought I'd teach them a few things about the solar system. Saturn's rings are made of billions of chunks of ice and that sort of thing. Maria might not let me. All she wants to hear is the story of Cinderella and the glass slipper. It fascinates her completely.'

'Don't forget to teach them that the word 'Mexico' means "the navel of the moon".'

Fact:

Mary Ann Cotton was born in 1822, near Durham, in the village of East Rainton. She was born to Michael and Margaret Robson. Her father was a pitman who was killed in a mine when Mary Ann was fourteen.

It was Dr Thomas Scattergood, a lecturer in forensic medicine and toxicology at Leeds Medical School, who proved that arsenical poisoning had caused the death of Mary Ann Cotton's victims, which included many of her children, stepchildren and husbands.

At that time, the Daily News *opined that 'Women have a natural turn for poisoning. Usually by arsenic.'*

There is white, grey, metallic arsenic, and arsenic troxide arsenous oxide and arsenic trihydride. In its pure and natural state it is grey metal. The element is found in enamels, paints, wallpapers, opal glass and traces are present in all human tissue. In homicidal or suicidal cases, arsenic is generally swallowed. It can also be inhaled as a dust or as arsine gas.

Mary Ann Cotton bought soft soap and arsenic for cleaning bedsteads and killing bedbugs. She said, 'I like to have a clean house.'

She argued that it must have been the green floral wallpaper covering the walls of her home that had accidentally poisoned everyone. She explained that she was never poisoned because she hated to touch walls.

'I hate walls. I cannot even lean against a wall,' she said. 'A wall is a horrible thing.'

At first chronic arsenic poisoning causes the victim to experience burning pains in the hands and feet and a numbing sensation throughout the body. Skin irritations, hair loss and visual impairment often follow these symptoms. Symptoms of arsenic poisoning begin as early as one half-hour after ingestion.

When Mary Ann was charged with murder she said, 'I am as innocent as the child unborn.'

Mary Ann Cotton died on the scaffold at Durham County Gaol at 8 a.m. on Monday, 24 March 1873. Her name was immortalised in a rhyme:

> *Mary Ann Cotton*
> *She's dead and she's rotten*
> *She lies in her bed*
> *With her eyes wide open.*
> *Sing, sing, oh, what can I sing?*
> *Mary Ann Cotton is tied up wi' string.*
> *Where, where? Up in the air*
> *Sellin' black puddings a penny a pair.*

17.

Well, She's Walking Through the Clouds

When Mexico City shuts down and windows and doors close against the dust-filled, dirty night, Emily and Santi lie in bed and talk. They know their voices better than their faces and bodies.

'I cannot see you,' Santi says. 'You're a river of milk.'

Santi can stay up all night talking for hours. Sometimes he behaves as if Emily isn't even there, but she understands this because she was also raised alone in a quiet house. One of the reasons that she loves to listen is that he tells her all kinds of facts and stories. He likes stories about shipwrecks and tells her about the collision between the *Stockholm* and the *Andrea Doria*. His favourite story is about the mystery of the *Mary Celeste*.

'This happened in 1872,' Santi explains. 'The *Mary Celeste* was deserted. Captain Briggs, his wife and daughter, and the ship's seven-member crew were nowhere to be found. The lifeboat was missing but all the crew's belongings were safely stowed in their quarters, implying a hasty evacuation of the ship. A half-eaten meal was on a table. Forks and knives were still placed within a ham. Some claimed that the food was warm.'

'Maybe you should have left me half-eaten meals in my room instead of arrowheads and my dress on the bed,' Emily answers.

'That's not a bad idea,' he answers. 'I should have thought of that. I did leave you some apples and I did leave your bed unmade, which could look like someone had to leave very quickly.'

'Actually,' Emily says, 'the more I think about what you did – living here and watching me – the more I realise that I was living the story of *The Three Bears*.'

'What do you mean?'

'Think about it,' Emily says and adds in a deep voice, 'Who's been sleeping in my bed?'

'Yes, I did sleep in your bed. It was as close as I could get to being with you.'

Santi finds Emily's knowledge about saints very amusing. She replies that he has Mother Agata to thank for that.

'You talk about them as if they were your family,' Santi says. 'I feel like they're your old aunts and uncles.'

'That's funny,' Emily answers. 'If they are my family, then they are your family also.'

'Who would be my aunt then?'

'I don't know,' Emily answers. 'Let me think . . .'

'Is there a saint for cousins?'

'I can't think of one,' Emily says. 'But there are saints for everything. I'll have to ask Mother Agata, she'll know.'

'I don't think that Mother Agata is going to like me very much. I think she's probably very possessive of you and wants to keep you for herself.'

'You can't say that. You don't even know her,' Emily protests. 'She's incredibly kind. I don't know what I would have done without her. There was never anyone to see for me. Only my father looked after me and made sure my hands were clean and that my right shoe was on my right foot. But Mother Agata talked to me. My father read me *Gulliver's Travels*, but Mother Agata walked me around the block.

'She's always worried about me, though. She says I'm a rag doll and smell like oatmeal – this is supposed to mean that I'm weak. She once told my father that she was worried that I was too isolated here. She wanted me to go off to school in the United States or in Britain. My father has always felt that this house and his company were enough. Mother Agata even scolds my father. Imagine! She once asked what had happened to the wild Cornish genes that brought our family to Mexico. She says that your father was pretty adventurous. Is this true?'

'My father described your father as "civilised". I am not sure this was a positive remark.'

'There is one more thing that I must tell you about Mother Agata,' Emily continues. 'Her life has been devoted to lost children. She harbours no ill will towards anyone or anything. She's a true Christian in that sense.'

One night, while Santi and Emily are lying in bed in her bedroom, he tells Emily about the tactics used by interrogators during the Inquisition.

It is late at night and they are eating some peeled apples and cashew nuts that Emily brought up to her bedroom earlier in the evening. She has been doing this every night for two weeks in case Santi gets hungry. She also brings up a large jug of water and two glasses.

'The questioner asked the victim each question in Latin and in the third person. But these questions had to be answered in the first person. This made the interrogations even more terrifying,' Santi explains. 'It created a kind of disassociation.'

'It must have made the victims feel that they were not there. As if they had overheard a conversation about themselves,' Emily answers. 'It makes me shudder.'

'Well, that was the point,' Santi says. He picks up a slice of an apple and chews it. He leans over and kisses Emily and pushes the pieces of apple from his mouth into hers.

Emily spits the lumps of apple into the palm of her hand. 'Don't do that, please,' she says.

'I was feeding you like a mother bird,' Santi answers, laughing softly. 'Does it disgust you?'

'I prefer to eat my own.'

Santi sits up in the bed with exaggerated stiffness, crosses his arms and throws his hair back with a snap of his head and frowns. 'I will be the Inquisition,' he says, getting to his feet. 'Let's play.'

Emily thinks he looks beautiful standing naked in the middle of her room. His body is slightly lit by the light that comes in through the window from the street lamp.

'OK,' Emily answers as she picks up the tray of nuts and apples and places it on the floor. 'Do you need to blindfold me?' she asks.

'We had not thought of that. This time we will not cover her face. We want to see her face,' Santi answers. 'Did Emily Neale confess to looking at the moon?' he continues in a deep, affected voice, 'Did she look at the moon?'

'No, I do not confess to anything and, yes, I have looked at the moon,' Emily answers, laughing.

'Did she look at the moon and then did Emily Neale look at the sun?' Santi asks again.

'Yes, sir. I have looked at both the sun and the moon.'

'Did she write in documents that the earth was not the centre of the solar system?' Santi questions. He walks toward her and kneels beside her on the bed. He presses his forehead against her forehead. Their eyes are so close that their eyelashes touch.

'I did say that, sir, but I never wrote it in a document, only in a letter to a friend. No, sir, I am not Galileo,' Emily adds with a smile. 'You thought I would not guess, didn't you, Santi?'

'Does Emily Neale confess to sexual intercourse with her

cousin? Does she confess to mixing her blood with her own blood?' Santi asks ignoring her question and continuing to play the game. 'Does she know that she could be stoned to death for this light-hearted fun and pleasure?'

'That's enough, Santi!' she stammers. 'You can stop this now,' she adds as she moves away from him and towards the edge of the bed. 'I don't think that's funny.'

Santi laughs out loud and says, 'Emily Neale does not like to play . . .'

'I don't like this game,' Emily whispers and shakes her head. 'Please stop.'

Santiago places his arm around her and pulls her back down beside him, 'Sorry. Sorry. Sorry,' he says. He repeats the word three times.

'Now, I'll ask you an easy question. Does Emily Neale know what rock band gave a personal concert for a Mexican president?'

'The Doors. That was easy.'

'Yes, too easy. Here's a question she cannot answer. What's my second name?'

'I don't know. Tell me.'

'Emily, are you a lucky person?'

'Mother Agata says that we must do whatever it takes to keep bad luck away. Do you cross your fingers? Do you knock on wood? Did you know that to wish someone luck is always unlucky? But,' Emily continues, 'you didn't answer. You didn't tell me your second name.'

Over their voices and breath they suddenly hear the telephone ring. The sound breaks into the dark room like a frightening alarm or siren. Emily gets up on her elbows and looks at the clock beside her bed. In the dark she is only just able to see that the hands point to five a.m. 'It's the orphanage,' Emily says. 'It's Mother Agata. Oh no,' she adds in a panicky voice. 'It's Angelica.'

'I don't have a second name,' Santi says.

Down the hall she can hear her father move out of his bed and pick up the telephone. Santi and Emily lie very still. A few seconds later they hear Emily's father open his bedroom door and walk down the hallway toward Emily's room.

They hear the quiet steps: one, two, three . . .

He knocks on the door and says softly, 'Emily, darling, wake up.'

Santi and Emily lie very still.

'What is it, father?' Emily calls out.

'It was Mother Agata,' he answers. 'She wants you to go over to the orphanage right away. The little girl, Angelica, is sick. Don't worry, I'll take you.'

'Yes, thank you,' Emily answers, getting out of the bed. 'I'll be ready in a few minutes.'

'I'll meet you downstairs,' Emily's father says and walks back to his room.

They hear the quiet steps: one, two, three . . .

'What's wrong?' Santiago whispers after a few seconds. 'Thank God he didn't open the door.'

'He's always very respectful. He never would have opened my door,' she answers. 'He always knocks.'

'So, tell me, what's the matter?' he whispers.

'It is one of the orphans. She's a strange and lovely little girl who was badly burned. She lost her parents in a fire. She's very brave.' Emily turns on the light and opens her closet door. 'She must be very sick for Mother Agata to call at this hour. I wonder what's happened.'

Santi leans back on the pillows, places his hands behind his head and watches Emily get dressed.

'Someday, when I'm sick, will you run like this to take care of me?' Santi asks.

'What? What did you say?' Emily replies as she searches through a drawer for a sweater. 'Poor child. It's so sad when the orphans get sick because that is when you realise how alone they really are. They don't belong to anyone. This little girl, Angelica, hates to be warm and is always looking for a cool place to lie down or something cool to drink. She's thirsty all the time – just like you, Santi. Just like you. Believe me, if you could see her and the burns all over her body your heart would break.'

'Listen to me. I asked you if you will run to take care of me someday?' Santi asks again.

'Of course,' Emily answers as she sits on the edge of the bed and ties up the laces of her shoes. 'Of course I would nurse you.'

'Then come over here and kiss me,' Santiago says.

Emily swivels, leans over and kisses him.

'I don't like you loving others,' Santi says. 'I only want you to love me. Nobody ever taught me to share.'

'That's because you're a spoiled child,' Emily says and laughs.

'Maybe so,' Santi answers. 'But don't you realise I'm jealous and I'm not joking. I am jealous of the clothes against your skin. I am jealous of the food you eat, jealous of the grape in your mouth, jealous of the cup against your lips . . .'

'Shhh. Quiet. My father will hear you in here,' Emily whispers.

Santi sit up in the bed. 'I'm jealous of the road you walk when you walk away from me,' he says.

'Shhh. Quiet.'

As Emily brushes her hair and ties it in a knot at the nape of her neck, he softly sings, almost humming, as he watches her. Emily knows the song:

> *Well, she's walking through the clouds*
> *With a circus mind that's running wild*
> *Butterflies and zebras and moonbeams and fairy tales*
> *That's all she ever thinks about*
> *Riding with the wind . . .*

After a pause, Santi stops. 'Listen,' he says. 'If you leave me I know what will happen – nothing will fit. I won't be able to put on my clothes and shoes. Everything will be too small.'

At the orphanage the atmosphere is very quiet since all the children are still asleep. Mother Agata greets Emily and her father at the front door. She is dressed in an old, brown bathrobe and her long grey hair is tied in two braids that fall over her shoulders and down over her arms. She continuously pulls on the braids as if they were bell ropes.

'Thank you for coming so quickly,' Mother Agata says in a loud whisper. 'Angelica is as sick as any child I've ever seen. It was just luck that I got up so early and decided to check on her. She was lying very still under the sheet saying "Angelica is hot, Angelica is hot", over and over again to herself. The doctor is here but I think she'd be very comforted to see Emily.'

'Of course,' Emily's father answers. 'Emily would not want to be anywhere else.'

'Dr Rodriquez has already gone upstairs,' Mother Agata says. She speaks in a panicked pitter-patter of words. 'Follow me. He's been here for twenty minutes now. I called him first, of course. Yesterday I was sure I saw the finger of God everywhere. I am terribly worried. I've made many vows. Poor child. If she lives I'll be an angel to her. She must be saved. How can a child get sick so quickly? Yesterday she was sitting on the patio and drawing. I watched her lay her cheek down on the cool piece of paper. I am terribly worried. Sweet Virgin Mary, console me.'

They quickly cross the dark courtyard and go up the stairs. As they approach Angelica's room the doctor opens the door and meets them in the hall. The hallway is lined with framed photographs that show the history of the orphanage. There are black and white ones that show Emily's great-grandmother with the building committee and the first teachers. There is also a photograph of 'Ye Olde English Fayre', which she organised to raise funds for the furnishing of the orphanage. It shows a group of women standing in a row dressed in Elizabethan costume. The walls are also covered with photographs of generations of children who were raised in the building. There is a photograph of her great-grandparents at Christ Church on 20 May 1910, when President Porfirio Diaz attended a memorial service for King Edward VII. At the end of the rows of pictures there is a photograph of Mother Agata with Emily's mother. They are standing in the patio against a lime-coloured wall with their arms around each other. Emily's mother's eyes are closed.

Dr Rodriguez has taken care of the children at the orphanage for over twenty years. He has also always been Emily's doctor.

'Angelica has a very high fever,' Dr Rodriquez explains, placing a thermometer into the pocket of his shirt and removing his eyeglasses. 'This can happen to burn victims even after one thinks that the worst is over. It is probably an infection somewhere in her skin. I'll go and call the hospital and let them know to expect her. Her pulse is very fast.'

'Can I go in and see her?' Emily asks.

'Of course,' the doctor replies. 'Tell her that she has to go to the hospital for a few days. Maybe you can pack a bag for her. Please allow me to call the hospital and let them know we're coming.'

'She isn't going to want to leave,' Mother Agata says. 'I don't know how we'll get her to agree to go to the hospital. She hates those places. She has spent most of her life in a hospital, poor child.'

'There's no choice,' Dr Rodriguez replies. 'She needs better care. She needs intravenous antibiotics immediately.'

'I'll see what I can do,' Emily answers.

'I'll take you to my office so you can call the hospital,' Mother Agata says to Dr Rodriguez. Emily can see that she is terribly upset since she keeps pulling at her braids over and over again and walking on tiptoe as if she were a child.

In the room Angelica is lying very still. Emily can make out the pulse of her fast heartbeat on the right side of her neck. Her eyes shine like small, wet stones. She looks tiny in the bed, like a small animal, a rabbit, a mouse.

Emily turns off the lamp beside the bed. She knows that Angelica hates light.

Emily sits down on the edge of her bed. Emily knows not to touch her, not to take her hand.

Angelica hates to be touched.

'I always wanted to learn how to speak finely,' Angelica whispers. 'I wanted to learn to speak nice, like you do, with words like "appreciate" and "if you don't mind".'

'You will,' Emily answers. 'It isn't difficult. You'll learn one day.'

Fact:

Vera Renczi was born in Bucharest in the early 1930s. She was a possessive and jealous woman who was convinced that all her husbands and lovers were unfaithful.

She said, 'If I saw one of my men even look at another woman that was it. If I saw him speak to another woman that was it. If I saw him talk to another woman that was it. Talking or speaking, that was it.'

Vera would not share her belongings with anyone. She would not share her hairbrush. She never allowed anyone to taste the food on her plate. She would never give away half an apple or a slice of orange. If she had sweets she would hide them in her pockets. If someone asked her for something she would say, 'I do not believe in lending or borrowing.'

She said that all the men in her life had abandoned her, even though she prepared romantic dinners for them with candles, music and good wine. However, when the police opened her wine cellar they found thirty-two male cadavers, each preserved in his own customised coffin.

Vera Renczi said that she was a great cook. She was proud of her recipes and she would not share them with anyone. If she were pressed, she'd give away modified recipes with one ingredient omitted, or with certain portions reduced or increased, so that nobody would be able to cook as well as she did.

This was her favourite recipe:

ONION DISH

Choose a few big, white onions. Clean and wash them. Boil over high heat until soft. Let them cool and then remove the core.

Make a stuffing of crushed walnuts, breadcrumbs dipped in milk, chopped onion cores, finely chopped fresh dill and parsley, and black olives – pits removed. Add salt and black pepper, according to taste. Also add a pinch of arsenic. Stuff the onions.

Place the onions in a pot and cover with the following sauce: mix flour, cooking oil, a cup of dry white wine and a few spoonfuls of sour cream. Also add a pinch of arsenic. Place the pot in the heated oven until the sauce thickens.

On Christmas or Easter serve with Cozonac bread.

18.

A Sad Day and a Sad Chapter

Angelica is buried on 13 June, the feast day of Saint Anthony of Padua.

In the morning, before the funeral, when Emily asks Santi if he wants to go with her, he says, 'No.' They are sitting in the kitchen having a breakfast of sliced papaya with lemon and salt and toast with butter and strawberry jam. The kitchen table is covered with a white cotton cloth embroidered with flowers.

'Why not?' Emily asks.

'No,' he answers.

'Why not?' Emily asks again.

'Because I didn't know her. Please, I don't, I can't . . .' he stammers.

'But why should that stop you? You know it means a lot to me. I loved her. Why don't you care, for my sake?'

'Listen, Emily,' Santi says very slowly as if there were a full stop after each word. 'Please don't ever try to convince me to do something I don't want to do.'

'I would have thought it was just a sort of basic human kindness,' Emily answered.

'I am not going to go and stand over a grave. It is not about kindness,' Santi adds firmly.

'This orphanage was founded by your family too. A fifth of the profits from the silver mine, remember?' Emily says crossly.

'My father and mother never talked about all of that. The past is not important.'

Emily's father arranges to have Angelica buried in the British cemetery. The cemetery is located on the broad Mexico Tacuba Avenue, which is flanked by the Spanish, Jewish, Portuguese, US and French cemeteries. These large areas of land were once on the outskirts of Mexico City. Large factories and warehouses have replaced the parklands that surrounded them. Along the avenue there are dozens of stores that sell marble and stone gravestones and offer engraving services. At every street corner there is a flower stand that bursts with red and white carnations with their stems seeping in large blue and white plastic buckets filled with murky water.

The cemetery is overgrown and poorly kept. Outside the main wrought iron gate there is a plaque that states that the first stone was laid in 1926. The small, round Anglican chapel that lies within the cemetery's land is a ruin of broken glass windows and cracked walls. A section of the roof has caved in and swallows have built nests in the ceiling. The birds swoop in and out of the shattered windows. The chapel smells like damp leaves.

Angelica is buried in a grave beside a Scotsman who died at sea in 1897 and an Englishman who died during the Second World War.

Emily's father rents one orange school bus so that all the orphans can go to Angelica's funeral. During the burial rites the children are very quiet. Each child solemnly takes a turn throwing a handful of dirt on Angelica's coffin. Afterwards, they run around the cemetery as if they were let loose to play in an enormous garden. Under rows of glossy privet trees they read the gravestones: Percy Porteous (World War Royal Field Artillery and Boer War Imperial Yeomanry) Killed in Mexico City, 8th June 1938, born in Sunderland, England 22 April 1884.

'The Japanese' quickly figure out that the tombs of children usually have small stone sculptures of angels above them. They hold hands and amble in and around the tombs and read aloud: Fuller, baby daughter, 23 March 1948; Barlow, baby son; *Niño* Meade; *Niño* Carlos J. O'Gorman; *Niña* Wallis, 16 August, 1919; and Anita, infant daughter of Frank and Anita Merron, January 1900.

'Learning one's ABCs, reading class, reading books, reading tombs, what's the difference?' Mother Agata asks in a defeated voice as she watches the orphans run around the graveyard.

Emily and Mother Agata sit on a green wrought iron

bench along the centre gravel path. 'It's windy,' Mother Agata says as she looks up at the trees.

'Yes,' Emily answers. She thinks today the city bears the name of *Mexico Tenochtitlan* – sad and cruel – the 'place of the fruit of the cactus'. 'It is odd to read the gravestones and see where everyone came from: Liverpool; Renfrewshire; Elgin in Scotland; Manchester . . . Did you see the one from Cornwall?' Emily continues.

'Yes, he must have been a miner, of course, or a brewer,' Mother Agata answers.

'We must be going, gather up the children,' Emily's father says, walking towards them down the gravel path. It moves Emily to see him dressed with such respect for Angelica in a dark blue suit with a black tie. For the first time, she understands that he is the only father all of these children have. He gives Emily his arm and she stands and takes it. They leave Mother Agata sitting on the bench as they walk together towards a cluster of gravestones on the east side of the cemetery.

'The Neales are buried here,' Emily's father says as he looks down on the carved stones surrounded by overgrown grass and azalea bushes.

They stand in silence and, after a few minutes, walk back towards Mother Agata and sit down beside her. Without speaking they watch as a few of the children lie down on the tombs, close their eyes and pretend they are dead.

Angelica is the first orphan Mother Agata has lost.

'She was a wounded animal, just a fragile wounded animal,' Mother Agata says again and again. She carries an enormous white handkerchief in her hand that looks more like a big white flag. She cannot stop crying and blowing her nose.

'You did the best that you could do,' Emily's father says to Mother Agata. He places his hand on her shoulder. 'Who knows what kind of life was in store for her. It wasn't going to be easy.'

'It is so hard to imagine the orphanage without her,' Emily replies. 'The place is going to feel so lonely.'

'Yes,' Mother Agata says. 'I remember the day she arrived. She was in my office and kept moving from one chair to another. Later I found out that this was because as soon as her body warmed something she had to move to find another cool place.'

'Yes, she was always doing that,' Emily adds.

'I remember after she'd been at the orphanage for a few days she said something very odd. She said that nobody understood time and that some days had three or four nights. Of course, she was right,' Mother Agata says.

'I remember how she would sit in a cold bathtub for hours. She never would eat anything and finally we figured out that it was painful for her to eat hot food,' Emily recalls. 'And she never said anything. She just wouldn't eat.'

'Yes, I remember.'

As she sits in the cool shaded graveyard listening to the sound of the children running around her and the trucks passing by on the avenue outside the wall, Emily thinks about Angelica's small burned hands, which were filled with pieces of melting ice or small cold pebbles. She remembers the day when nobody could find Angelica. Everyone in the orphanage was asked to look for her. Even the other orphans ran around looking in closets and under the staircases. Finally, Emily found her standing in the kitchen in front of the refrigerator. Angelica stood naked with the door hanging wide open. The light from inside the refrigerator lit up the girl's frail and scarred body.

The cousins, Hipolito and Maria, are the orphans most affected by Angelica's death. They walk around the cemetery with their arms around each other and at a distance from the other children. At one point they sit down under a tree. From a distance, Emily watches as Maria strokes Hipolito's hair, kisses his cheek and places her fingers in his mouth.

When Emily gets home from the funeral she marches past Santi, who is at the dining room table working on some architectural drawings. He chews on a pencil in his mouth as if it were a cigar. He is listening to the news on his portable radio. He calls out to Emily as she walks in, 'Hello there. How did it go?'

Emily does not answer. She walks past him and runs upstairs to her bedroom. When she opens the door she comes to a quick stop and holds her hands over her heart. There are three white roses on her bed. Santi has arranged them in such a way that they spell out the letter 'A'. 'A' for Angelica. She thinks it makes her bed look like a tomb.

Emily cautiously picks up the roses at the base of their stem so she does not prick her fingers and places them on the floor beside the rubbish bin. She's confused. She doesn't know if this is nice or not. She's not ready to forgive.

In the room Emily can also see that some of the remnants of the night before still permeate her bedroom. Santi's sweater lies over a chair and she can see that his shoes, which he quickly kicked off his feet, are still under her bed. There is a bottle of tequila on her dresser and two shot glasses on the table by her bed. Her stockings and silk blouse rest on a chair.

The room smells like melons and rice water.

She can still hear the conversation they had last night linger in the room: *Cousin. Yes, yes, I know. Charles Darwin wed his cousin Emma. Albert Einstein's second wife Elsa was his cousin. Yes, yes, I know. Queen Victoria married her cousin. Europeans have always married their cousins. In the United States the marriage of cousins is banned in twenty-four states. Yes, yes, I know. Jacob married his first cousins, Rachel and Leah. Yes, yes, I know. Isaac and Rebekah were cousins. The Roman Catholic Church opposes cousin marriages and only gives compensation to couples considered worthy. Cousin. Yes, yes, I know. Kissing cousin. Kinsman. Kinsfolk. A Cousin Betsy is a half-witted person. Yes, yes, I know. Consanguinity. No man shall marry his mother, grandmother, daughter, granddaughter, stepmother, grandfather's wife, son's wife, grandson's wife, wife's mother, wife's grandmother, wife's daughter, wife's granddaughter, nor his sister, brother's daughter, sister's daughter, father's sister, or mother's sister, or cousin of the first degree. No woman shall marry her father, grandfather, son, grandson, stepfather, grandmother's husband, daughter's husband, granddaughter's husband, husband's father, husband's grandfather, husband's son, husband's grandson, nor her brother, brother's son, sister's son, father's brother, mother's brother, or cousin of the first degree. Yes, yes, I know. Cousin-German. Cousin Jack. Inbreeding. Yes, we're all cousins, that's what I believe, because we're all children of Adam and Eve . . . But we're kissin' cousins 'n' that'll make it all right. Yes, yes, that's Elvis Presley!*

Fact:

My name is Debra Sue Tuggle and I was born in Little Rock, Arkansas, in 1958. People say that they've heard me say things that I have never said. I never said that pressing a pillow over a child's face stopped the creature from crying and I did not do that to five children. I'm innocent.

Some people said that they'd heard me speaking to myself when I was shopping at the supermarket or walking down the street and I never talk to myself. I am not a crazy lady!

Someone asks why do you kill? Well, I say you never know why you kill. It is like being hungry or thirsty. It is like that feeling of wanting an apple or a chocolate and you just have to have it. Sometimes it's just the look on someone's face that gives you that

desire. Or it's the weather or because you're tired or just anything
at all. No person likes to admit it, but I admit it.

    Listen, this is the truth. I know there are many wives out there
who pray their husbands' aeroplanes will fall from the sky when
their men are away on business trips. They won't admit it, but it
is true. The wives are counting the money; they're thinking about
their freedom. They're planning what they will do with their
husbands' things and how they'll have more space in the house for
their own belongings. They imagine their houses without suits, ties
and shirts in them. They can see themselves throwing away razors,
shaving cream and toothbrushes. And throwing away those big fat
wood hangers that are especially made for men's suit jackets. They
can see themselves calling up the Salvation Army to ask them to
pick up some stuff, men's stuff.

19.

A Visit with the Gods

Emily sits at the dining room table and watches Santi work on his architectural drawings. She presses her hands on the wood and thinks about how the table crossed the Atlantic Ocean from Britain to Mexico. She can imagine British sailors carrying it down a gangplank into the port city of Veracruz. She can also visualise it being placed on a train and transported to Mexico City. Along the length of oak are stains, grooves and marks from generations of use. On one corner there are ringed marks from water glasses and on one side there is a mark where someone with a butter knife once carved in the letter 'o' or the shape of a circle into the golden wood. Emily has never been able to tell which one it is – a circle or the letter – but her index finger has traced it over and over again throughout her whole life – around and around. In the centre of the table there is a blue hand-blown glass pitcher filled with bougainvillea branches that are bursting with deep pink flowers that look as if they are made of crepe paper.

Santi has just had a shower and he is dressed in only a light blue terrycloth bathrobe and is barefoot. He hates to wear shoes. As soon as he gets home the first thing he does is to take off his socks and shoes or boots. Emily thinks he smells fresh – a combination of rose soap and mint-scented shaving cream. Santi says that he loves to work after taking a shower. 'It is a habit left over from living in Chihuahua and that heat,' he explains. 'A cool shower allows you to think.'

Santi is designing a Baptist church for a group of missionaries from Texas. He has two pencils stuck in his black, wavy hair. Emily sits beside him and watches him draw lines on the large pieces of white paper. For paperweights he uses red apples from the kitchen. His freckled hands hold the rulers and pencils with confidence.

'They want something austere. Nothing that might reek of Catholicism,' Santi says as he takes a sip from a tall glass of hibiscus flower water.

'Yes, I can imagine. Something like a warehouse with square windows. That's just what my father always complains about,' Emily says. 'He claims that architects are ruining this city. He's right. Beautiful buildings are torn down daily and ugly ones are built in their place. He told me an interesting story about the Cornish miners in Pachuca. When they built their Methodist church up in the mining town of Real del Monte, the Mexicans were shocked because it was such a plain, boring building. For Catholics, this was inexplicable.'

Every now and again, as he continues to draw, Santi looks

up at Emily. He picks up an eraser and rubs out a dark pencilled line on the paper.

'In fact,' Emily adds, 'I thought my father was going to throw you out of this house when he heard you were an architect. He hates architects.'

'Architecture expresses the time.'

'Yes,' Emily agrees. 'But whole neighbourhoods have been ruined.'

'If everything stayed the same, architects would have no work and they would not be able to earn a living,' Santi explains as he reaches for a long metal ruler.

'Yes, architects always say that. But the fact remains that they have destroyed this city,' Emily says. She takes a sip of Santi's glass of hibiscus flower water and asks, 'Do you miss working on the ranch in Chihuahua? Do you miss that kind of life?'

'Yes, I miss it sometimes. But it was lonely, a lonely life for a boy,' Santi answers, chewing on the end of one of his pencils. 'Actually, you know what I do miss? I miss horses. I loved the horses and I enjoyed breaking them in.'

'You broke in horses? How did you do it? You've never mentioned this,' Emily answers surprised. 'I've never even ridden a horse.' Emily thinks that there is still so much they really don't know about each other.

'Your body has to connect to the horse. This is the only way to do it. You have to stand close to the animal and speak to it. I also spend a large amount of time around the horse doing other things until it gets to know me. Sometimes I'd just sit in a stall beside the wild horse reading a book. I'd do this for days and days,' Santi explains.

'What do you say? What do you talk to the horse about?'

'That's a secret. Some people like to exhaust them or dominate them into submission. There are horse trainers who are very violent. My father was a bit too heavy-handed for my taste. He believed in the whip.'

'Why is what you tell a horse a secret?'

'Well, not really a secret. It's true that some people are very secretive about what they say to their horses. Actually, in my case, I just tell the horse whatever comes to my mind. I sing songs all the time or whistle. Sometimes I tell the horse, "You're mine, you're mine, you're mine."'

'You must have felt so free there.'

'Chihuahua?' Santi asks. 'It was so hot and dry. A place for hornets and wasps. Sometimes I'd ride out into the desert, but it was pretty unbearable. I'd go before sunrise, leaving in the dark. It was so hot that everything in the house creaked. It was as though the wooden chairs and tables were about to break from lack of water. It was a noise one never got used to. It was particularly bad at night, when the cooler air made the wood shrink and the whole house sounded like it was shattering. I once had a guitar that literally broke into two pieces.'

Santi stands up and, holding his silver-coloured metal ruler in one hand and hitting it against his other hand, he walks towards her. Emily thinks he is going to strike her.

'What are you doing?' she asks, frowning and walking backwards away from him. 'Is something the matter?'

'You say that our mouths are exactly the same,' he says as he stands in front of her, takes hold of her wrist and pulls her towards him. 'Let's see if it is true, Cousin Emily. I want to know the architecture of your body. Where are your windows, floors and doors? Where is the sanctuary?'

He presses the cold metal ruler over her mouth.

'Two and a half inches,' he says as he reads the numbers along the ruler. Then, he places the ruler on his face and measures his own mouth.

'Yes,' Santi says. 'Two and a half inches. You're right, our mouths are identical.'

'But they don't taste the same. Or do they?'

'No, you taste like my hands,' Santi says as he places two fingers in her mouth.

A few days later Emily takes Santi to visit the pyramids of Teotihuacán. Since he grew up far north in Chihuahua he has never seen them. Emily packs a picnic lunch for the day trip.

As they step out of the house and walk across the pavement to get into her car, Emily realises that this is the first time they have been out of the house together. She lifts her face to the open space of sky and sun above them and feels the heat and movement of Santi's body beside her body. It is as if the space from the front door to her car is an enormous field.

Teotihuacán is forty kilometres north of Mexico City. It takes over an hour and a half just to get out of the city after a voyage through corridors of huge cement trucks, petrol trucks, massive trailers that choke the air with diesel fumes, buses and thousands of cars spewing black and blue smoke. As they drive they read the names of trucks that Mexican truck drivers paint on the back of their vehicles above the licence plate or above a back tyre. The names make them laugh: Mighty Mouse; Heart Slayer; Grandmother; Vengeance.

'We'll climb the Pyramid of the Sun,' Emily says as she drives the car through the traffic. 'The Pyramid of the Moon is too dangerous. Every so often people actually die by falling down its steep stairs. Or do you really feel like climbing both?'

'No, just one sounds fine to me.'

When they reach the highway and the traffic begins to move, Santi reaches over and places his hand on Emily's neck. As they begin to drive through the countryside they notice pepper trees, enormous yuccas and thickets of prickly pears lining the road. Also, along the side, there are dozens of white crosses that mark the site of fatal road accidents.

'It feels good to be moving, to be out of your father's house,' he says. 'It also is nice to get out of the city.'

'Yes,' Emily answers.

'A highway always makes me feel good. Shall I sing you a song? What would you like me to sing?'

'I don't know,' Emily answers. 'What songs do you know?'

'I've memorised hundreds of songs. Actually, I don't really need to memorise them. Once I hear a song, I just know it.'

After a short pause, he quietly begins to sing. His voice is a beautiful tenor. He draws each note out and fills the car with his voice. He sings the first verse of a revolutionary song that is from the State of Chihuahua and is called *La Valentina*:

> *I am dominated by a passion,*
> *Which is what has made me take you;*
> *Valentina, Valentina*
> *I wish to tell you.*

'Please keep singing it,' Emily begs him.

Santi continues and sings the songs most famous lines:

> *Valentina, Valentina,*
> *I kneel at your feet*
> *If they are going to kill me tomorrow*
> *Let them kill me right now.*

When he finishes he says to Emily, 'So many very good revolutionary songs came out of Chihuahua. Now, you sing something.'

'I can't sing. I can dance, though. Can you dance?' Emily asks. She thinks again about how little they really know each other. She believes that their bodies knew each other instantly.

'What do you think?' Santi asks. 'Of course I can dance! All the girls want to dance with me.'

When they arrive in Teotihuacán they park the car in a parking lot covered with a carpet of red gravel cut from volcanic rock. They decide to skip the small market outside the museum where there are dozens of stalls with people blowing glass and selling glass objects that include menageries of tiny animals: armadillos, snakes, rabbits, giraffes and lions. They decide not to visit the museum, but go directly to the Road of the Dead that leads straight to the pyramids.

As they walk, Santi takes hold of Emily's hand. 'It is so dry here. It's like being in the desert again,' Santi says.

'From what I understand, all the forests were cut down and the city was completely paved from pyramid to pyramid,' Emily explains. 'There isn't a single tree, is there?'

'What I like best about being here is that there's nobody here to see us,' he says. 'Well, maybe just some ancient gods.'

'Yes,' Emily answers. 'But they are the cruellest gods of all.'

'Do you think so?' he asks, placing his arm around her waist.

'The great god was Quetzalcoatl. There are many stories about him, but the most interesting story of all is that he fell into a trap. It's a story of incest and it's also one of Mexico's founding myths.'

'What was the trap?'

'He was tricked by his enemies into drinking too much alcohol and, confused and drunk, he seduced his elder sister, Quetzalpetlatl. When Quetzalcoatl realised what he had done he felt such horror that he went into self-imposed exile. He was supposed to have been pure and noble. Apparently, he even practised self-sacrifice and bled himself from many different parts of his body.'

'What happened to his sister?'

'I don't know. The legends never talk about her.'

When they get to the Pyramid of the Sun they climb the narrow steps in a zigzag angle – from left to right. From the top they survey the dry, distant tree-less landscape and stare down at the ancient city's twenty square kilometres, which are laid out in a grid pattern of temples, squares and residential housing.

'Isn't it amazing?' she says as she sits down on the summit. 'To think that so many people were sacrificed up here to spill their blood as food for the sun. The priests used to wear the skins of their victims like a ceremonial robe.'

'Yes,' Santi answers. 'I've read a little bit about that.'

'It is strange to imagine these steps covered with blood. It's said that there were hundreds of thousands of vultures that used to feed off of these stones. Did you know that some sacrifices even called for children? Of course, there is still so much we don't know. Archaeologists say that in this land there were three souls: one based in the heart, one in the liver and one in the head,' Emily explains. 'I think that the most frightful thing of all was that babies were forced to cry by being tortured. They thought that the tears of children would make the rain god happy and bring rain.'

'Yes, I can hear them,' Santi answers as he cups his hands over his ears.

'What do you mean?' Emily answers.

'Just imagine,' Santi says. 'Don't you feel it? This is a strange place.'

Santiago stands up. He looks pale. 'Let's leave,' he says and moves quickly towards the stairs.

'Yes, yes, of course,' Emily answers. She tries to take Santi's hand, but he gently pushes her away.

'Don't go so fast,' Emily calls out as she watches him charge down the steps in a confused manner. 'It is most dangerous going down,' she adds, stumbling behind him.

When Emily gets to the bottom of the pyramid, Santi is way ahead of her and marching down the Road of the Dead towards the car park. She takes a deep breath and follows him as quickly as she can. She is amazed at how quickly he can move and how far away he is from her in such a short period of time. As she walks she notices thin slivers and small square pieces of obsidian on the ground. She also sees hundreds of large red fire ants stirring in the ancient dirt.

A few minutes later, when Emily finally catches up with Santi, he is already in the car park sitting on the ground in the little piece of shadow that is cast by the car. He squats with his head resting on his knees.

'Are you all right?' Emily asks breathlessly.

'Yes,' Santi answers as he looks up at her. 'I feel better now. It is so hot here. Too hot.'

Emily leans over him and runs her fingers back and forth through his hair. The moisture from his scalp wets her fingertips.

'I just suddenly felt very sick,' Santi answers. 'I'm so sorry.'

Emily rubs her fingers along his cheek. 'Do you want something to drink?' she asks.

'No,' Santi answers and kisses the inside of Emily's hand, right in the centre of her palm. 'I wonder how you can talk about the sacrifices so calmly,' he continues. 'Doesn't it affect you? Especially what was done to the children?'

'They're just facts. Historical facts.'

'That's a cold-blooded answer,' he says with disgust.

'It's just, just history,' Emily whispers almost to herself and moves away from him. 'Of course it isn't very nice, but sacrifice was something beautiful to them.'

'Then you don't know very much about history,' Santi answers. 'These kinds of things are happening as we speak. Maybe my mother was right about me after all. She always said I was too sensitive. As a child I used to cry every time I walked past a butcher's shop and looked at the skinless carcasses of cows, pigs and rabbits hanging from those vicious metal hooks. My mother walked for blocks and blocks out of the way to avoid going near that place since it upset me so much.'

'She was kind,' Emily answers.

'Yes, but my father thought I was a coward.' Santiago stands up, takes the car keys from Emily and opens the car door. 'Let's go have our picnic,' he says as he brushes the red dust of the volcanic stone from his trousers. 'I'll drive now.'

'Do you really feel like it or should we just go home?' Emily asks as she gets into the car.

'I remember the sign over the door. It said "Jubilation". That's what that God damned butcher's shop was called: Jubilation.'

Fact:

Myra Smith said, 'My fucking idol is Bonnie Baxter!'

Myra Smith said, 'The greatest love story on earth is the love that Bonnie had for Clyde.'

Myra Smith said, 'I've never found my "Clyde", but I am still looking. And I'll never stop!'

She knew everything there was to know about Bonnie Baxter and kept all the facts about her in a small, leatherbound notebook. Myra Smith also kept a diary where she would write to Bonnie directly.

Myra Smith's Diary

Page 1

Bonnie baby, I love you! You are my machine-gun baby moll! You always said you wanted to be a poet and you are a poet! I'm jealous of your love and your little body and your number 5 glove size. I'm jealous of your blue eyes. Bonnie baby, you could have been my friend for sure and you could've permed my hair and done my nails. We would have gotten pretty together.

Page 2

You and Clyde always made love in the back seat of a car, a Ford V-8, which was better than a bed. Isn't that what you said to somebody?

Didn't you say when you make love in a car, under a tree, in a big cornfield, you feel like a man really loves you?

Page 3

Bonnie honey, you are a poet. Just like I told you already. "The Story of Suicide Sal" is the best poem ever! My favourite part is:

> You've heard of a woman's glory
> Being spent on a 'downright cur',
> Still you can't always judge the story
> As true, being told by her.

What does that mean, baby? Does that mean you were telling lies about everything to everybody? I really wish we could talk.

I love to read your letters too.

Clyde wrote you once from Waco Jail, 'I'm jealous of you and can't help it. And why shouldn't I be? If I was as sweet as you are to me, you would be jealous too.'

I'm jealous too. We could've been sisters, just you and me. You'd of let Clyde kiss me too, but after he'd kissed you, of course.

Page 4

What do you do when you love someone who is dead?

Page 5

Hey, you, 'pal of a killer', reckless lady, today I cooked up some red beans and cabbage, just what you always liked to eat.

Page 6

I was thinking, when you got so burned in that car crash and almost died, why didn't Clyde buy some butter and put it on your leg, arm and face? I should've been there to protect you. I know how to be a good nurse.

Bonnie, sweet little lady, I love you.

I wish you'd of been my sister, my little sister, my little lamb.

Page 7

I've not killed nobody. Not yet.

20.

Page 108 can be a Child Lost in the Forest

Emily and Santi drive for half an hour, past alfalfa fields and a large beer brewery, until they get to a small town, which is ugly and nondescript except that it contains the Monastery of the Dwarves. This is a seventeenth-century monastery built for the malformed children born to rich families. Thick walls surround a large garden, which contains a long walkway, flanked by several benches. Next to the building there is a graveyard with small, child-sized graves and tombstones. The monastery contains a small church, little rooms and a diminutive inner courtyard.

'It is Snow White's house,' Santiago says as they walk through the building.

'Yes, of course it is,' Emily answers. 'You're right. I never thought of that.'

'Tell me about this place,' Santi asks, taking Emily's hand in his as they walk towards the monastery. 'I'm so lucky to have a historian as a guide.'

'You know more about the building than I do,' Emily answers.

'Yes, I know about the columns and materials and all of that, but you know about the lives that were lived within them,' Santi says.

'I can tell you one thing I find interesting about studying seventeenth-century history. At that time, there were no attempts to hide what things were. Today we attempt to make things pretty, so nice-nice. In those times, places were given their brutal, honest names, like calling this the "Monastery of the Dwarves". Hospitals used to have names like the "Hospital of the Five Plagues". One museum in Mexico City was called the "Museum of Strange Objects",' Emily explains. 'I would have loved to have visited that museum. Someone told me at the university that the museum had the skeleton of a human hand with seven fingers.'

'Did they tell you anything else?'

'Yes, apparently one of the strange objects was a finger-nail that was ten inches long.'

'Historians are very strange people,' Santi says with a laugh.

Santiago and Emily have to bend over in order to be able to pass under the doorways and stand inside the small cells that were the bedrooms.

'Few people know about this place,' Emily says. 'It's quite a secret. My father says that my mother used to like to come here.'

'Do you remember your mother?'

'No, not really. I was only a baby. I do remember the smell of the rice powder she used on her face. But Mother Agata says that it's impossible for me to remember anything about her. I was too little, she says, to have built memories. My mother is something far away, like a dream that I can't remember but I can still feel.'

In one of the small, dark monk cells Santiago embraces Emily and kisses her neck.

'What are we going to do, Cousin Emily?' he asks.

'I don't know.'

'I am not going to leave you. Is it only your father who stops you? Do you care about anything else? If your father died would you stay with me? I am not going to leave you.'

'Just give me a little time,' Emily whispers.

'How much time do you need, a week?' Santi asks with his face still pressed against her neck.

'No. More than that.'

Santi moves away from her and walks out into the inner courtyard. Emily follows behind him. They both squint in the sunlight after being in the darkness of the monks' small, damp rooms. Emily links her arm through Santi's arm and guides him out to the garden. Under a tall eucalyptus tree they lay down a blanket in the shade. Emily opens the bag of lunch she had packed up that morning.

'I was in the library this morning looking at all the books. It's incredible to think that they were brought over here on a ship. Actually, what's incredible is they thought the books were so important,' Santi says, leaning back on his elbows.

'Our great-grandfather liked to read. My father says that he also brought over trunks filled with things to give away.'

'What kind of things?'

'I think there were quilts for the mining families and seeds, of course. If you go to Real del Monte some houses have English roses in their gardens. I think there were seeds going back and forth between Mexico and Britain all the time. I don't know if any Mexican plants took over there . . .'

'Have you read all those books?'

'No, but I've at least looked at all of them. There wasn't much else to do in the house. All I heard all day long was the sound of pages turning and books opening. Of course, thanks to my father, I also learned a lot about butterflies.'

'My upbringing was so different to yours. Sometimes I feel like I left more behind than I took away.'

'Mother Agata says that once my mother disappeared my father never looked the same. He developed a lack of will and fight. She says his skin even turned yellow as if it were dried between the leaves of a book like a four-leaf clover.'

'I'm sure your mother didn't disappear. Something happened to her. It may not have been bad.'

'I don't think I'll ever know,' Emily says.

She hands Santi two bottles of beer and a bottle opener.

'Did you see those hilarious books on hygiene?' Emily asks.

'No. I missed those.'

'Well, there are several books there by a Frank Overton. One is titled *General Hygiene* and the other is called *Personal Hygiene*. I can quote whole passages from them.'

'OK, tell me some . . .'

Emily sits up straight and pretends to declaim, 'A shoe which fits the right foot will not fit the left. When your clothes are afire, the first thing to do is to lie down. Many persons are wounded by stepping on nails and other sharp things which lie on the ground.'

'I can just imagine you all alone reading these hilarious things,' Santi laughs.

'Well, I was terrified, I kept wondering when my clothes were going to be afire. There is another book that I love called *Encyclopaedia of Mother's Advice*. It opens with an engraving that represents, and I quote, "the method of dividing an ox for the table and the manner of cooking those parts". And it has gems like: pounded glass mixed with corn-meal will keep rats away.'

'I suppose the rats ate the broken glass?'

'I suppose,' Emily agrees. 'The advice on how to be beautiful is so marvellously easy. It says, very simply, that the whole secret to being attractive is to throw up your chin.'

'So, Cousin Emily,' Santi asks as he leans against the tree with his arms crossed and looks towards the monastery. 'Is there a saint for dwarves?'

'No, not specifically for dwarves, that I know of,' Emily

answers. 'There's a saint for the physically disabled. He is Saint Giles.'

'What was his story?'

'He was wounded by an arrow when he tried to protect himself from a group of hunters.'

'So,' Santi asks, 'do you think that the dwarves who lived here prayed to Saint Giles?'

'I don't know. They probably did. Or they prayed to the saint of leg disorders since they were so small.'

'What!' Santi exclaims with disbelief. 'There's a saint for leg disorders?'

'Absolutely,' Emily replies. 'He is Servatius. He's also invoked against vermin.'

'I can't understand how you remember all these facts about the saints. How do you do it?'

'They're like real people to me. I feel like I know them. Just as you have no trouble memorising songs, these people's lives are easy for me to recall.'

'The stories are so unbelievable.'

'I was thinking,' Emily says. 'My father told me that his mother could remember all the songs that she had ever heard. He said she only ever had to hear a song one time to know it by heart. Maybe you get that from her . . .'

'My father never told me about that. But he may also have had the gene too since my father knew every song you can imagine. He even knew some naughty ditties from World War II.'

Emily opens the large plastic bag and takes out their lunch.

'How can you eat fucking cucumber sandwiches in Mexico? It's absurd!' Santi says as Emily hands him a plate. 'And,' he adds, 'why do you call yourself Emily? Your name should be Emilia. I think I'll call you Emilia from now on.'

Fact:

Someone can brand your arm or leg, like a cow or a horse.

The shape of brands for cattle are: diamond, X; box X; circle X; bar X; rocking X; swinging X; tumbling X; walking X; flying X; crazy P; lazy P; and reverse P.

A branding iron can be made in the shape of a heart.

The González Valenzuela sisters were known as the 'Poquianchis'. Their names were Delfina and María de Jesús. They had a whorehouse in downtown Mexico City, which was called 'The Happy House'.

Regarding the Poquianchis sisters, some people said that one had horns growing out of her head and that the other had feathers growing out of her skin.

The Happy House had torture rooms where the Poquianchis sisters punished the girls who worked for them. They branded their prostitutes on the left forearm. Some people said that the brand was in the shape of a heart. A few witnesses said that the brand was a letter of the alphabet and others said it was a number. Nobody remembers for sure. Some newspapers claimed that the branding was actually made up and that it never happened.

In the inside courtyard, lined with clay pots filled with azaleas, the sisters had their own cemetery. A secret cemetery. When the police went to The Happy House and had the ground in the centre courtyard of the house opened with pick axes and shovels they found over three hundred women's skeletons. The remains showed signs of beatings and starvation. They found children's skeletons. They found: tiny, small, diminutive, miniature, little, petite, baby femurs.

The González Valenzuela sisters knew that if you said someone had disappeared, it did not mean that they had died. They said that many girls just ran away, just ran away; they just disappeared, just disappeared; or they just went missing, went missing.

21.

Step on a Crack Breaks Your Mother's Back

The rainy season in Mexico City begins with the far-off sound of thunder, which can last for days. Then, every afternoon, the skies turn a blackish green and torrents of water drench the pink, blue, green, red and yellow walls. Frequently it hails and everyone watches the miracle of white stones as they fall from the sky. During the rains fountains overflow, statues turn green with moss and the lights go out. Every house in Mexico City has a drawer filled with candles.

Emily has not been back to the orphanage since Angelica's death. It has been a week. Emily dreads the emptiness of Angelica's dark room and small bed and the absence of a girl who ran away from the sun and bowed her head in reverence to the light of a lamp.

The courtyard is empty. The orphanage is quiet. Somebody has left a pair of red tennis shoes under a bench. At one side of this bench there are several child-sized brooms, mops and buckets.

She glances over at the large poplar tree where she used to read books to Angelica in the shade of its full branches. Emily remembers when a sliver of sun moved through the tree and landed on Angelica; the little girl squirmed and tried to hide under her arm. Emily remembers teaching Angelica the English word for ice.

Emily goes upstairs to Mother Agata's office and knocks on the door.

'Come in,' Mother Agata calls out. 'Who's there?'

Emily opens the door. Mother Agata sits at her desk in the large, throne-like chair she had custom made years ago. It even has red velvet upholstery as if it were a chair for a bishop. Emily thinks she looks like an enormous stone god.

Mother Agata studies a calendar spread out across her desk beside a stack of hymnbooks and a Bible. In her hand she holds a pencil that looks like a toothpick in her large fingers. Her long braids are tied up and form a crown pinned around the top of her head. She is drinking a tall glass of rice water.

'Where have you been? Sit down,' Mother Agata says. 'I'm checking next month's saints' days.'

Emily sits down in a chair in front of Mother Agata's desk. She has spent her whole life in this chair. She thinks of how she has grown up within the two armrests and recalls when her feet would dangle and could not touch the ground. The chair suddenly seems as familiar to her as her own body. She knows its curves and weight.

'Sometimes I think you are the only person left on earth who cares about saints' days,' Emily says.

'That's not true, many people care. Don't you listen to the radio? It tells you what saint's day it is every morning and evening,' Mother Agata replies.

'Do you have a favourite saint?'

'Of course. The most important saint of all is Saint Jude Thaddeus. Don't you agree? The most important saint has to be the saint of hopeless causes. You know that murderers, robbers and drug dealers always pray to him.'

'Some day we'll have to go to the San Hipolito church,' Mother Agata adds. 'I've never been there and I'm curious to go.'

'Yes,' Emily answers. 'I've never been either.'

The 500-year-old San Hipolito church is the place in Mexico City where Saint Jude is revered. On the twenty-eighth of every month hundreds of people go to pray to him. The police are said to keep the church under surveillance since so many criminals go there to worship.

'Where are the children?' Emily asks. 'The place is so silent and the courtyard was empty as I walked in. Did you send them all off somewhere?'

'Yes, they're on a field trip. They've gone to visit the zoo in Chapultepec Park. You know, I like them to go at least once a year so that they don't think they are better or superior to an animal. I've thought up a new game for them. I'll ask them what animal they think they look like.

Then they can draw a picture of themselves with the animal.'

'They'll love that,' Emily answers. 'I wonder what Hipolito and Maria will say?'

'Oh, they already know. They said that they did not need to go to the zoo to find out. Hipolito said he was an elephant. Maria said she was a kangaroo.'

'That's funny. They do sort of look like an elephant and a kangaroo . . .'

'What animal do you think you look like?'

'I don't know,' Emily says and touches her face. 'I've never thought about it before. I guess that, off-hand, I think I look like a white rabbit.'

'I'm a donkey,' Mother Agata answers. 'I've always known that.'

Emily laughs out loud.

'Don't laugh, Emily Neale,' Mother Agata says sternly, but with a smile. 'I'm perfectly serious. I mean it. I look like a donkey. I was also made to carry things. Taking care of all these children is like carrying sacks of firewood on my back!'

Emily stands up and walks over to the window and looks down on the empty patio. From above she sees two dead birds with yellow feathers lying within a tree's branches. She moves closer to the window and presses her face against the windowpane. On closer inspection Emily realises that the birds are actually two Barbie dolls, which a child must have thrown up into the tree.

'How are the children doing? Do they miss Angelica very much?' Emily asks.

'It's been terrible. I can't deny it. I've told them that she's with her mother and father in heaven and that seems to comfort them. This is the only hope the little orphans have, after all,' Mother Agata says as she crosses herself with her right hand. She bends her index finger over her thumb so that her fingers also make the shape of a cross. 'One word keeps coming to my mind. It is solace. It is such a beautiful word. I wish I could find solace.'

'Angelica was special,' Emily answers.

'Yes. Every time I go to the kitchen and open the refrigerator I think of her. Every morning I used to take her a piece of ice to suck on. There wasn't anything she liked better than a piece of ice.'

'I was thinking about that the other day. Do you remember when she thought she could get inside a refrigerator and didn't know how dangerous that would be?'

'Thank God you found her. And yet she died anyway . . .'

'So, tell me, what saint's day will you celebrate next month?' Emily asks as she turns from the window and sits down again. 'Will it be Mary, Thomas or Benedict?'

Mother Agata claps her large hands, which look more like two golden cymbals. The noise they make is large and full.

'Well done!' Mother Agata laughs, 'You're getting very good at this.'

'You made sure of that,' Emily replies.

'Well, I did a good job. I think I'll teach the children about Saint Thomas this month. What do you think? Of course he is Doubting Thomas and they love to hear about that – about a doubter. He didn't believe in the resurrection until he had touched Christ's wounds.'

'Don't you think it's a little difficult?' Emily asks. 'The concept of doubting is not that easy. Do you think that the thought of someone touching someone else's wounds is frightening?'

'I've never believed in over-protecting the children. Fear is a very large part of life. We are all so afraid of many things. I have never believed in hiding from what it is you fear.'

'What are you afraid of?' Emily asks as she leans closer to Mother Agata across the table.

'I cannot speak it, I cannot say it. The word does not fit in my mouth. What about you?'

Emily is quiet for a few seconds. She crosses her fingers. 'I'm afraid of what might have happened to my mother,' Emily says quietly.

'Yes, dear.'

'I wonder if we'll ever know . . .'

'You still cross you fingers?' Mother Agata asks as she looks at Emily's and points at her hands.

'You taught me to do anything possible to keep bad luck away. What superstitions do you continue to practise?'

'Oh, many,' Mother Agata answers, laughing. 'I can't help

it. My mother taught them to me: seagulls are the spirits of dead sailors; step on a crack breaks your mother's back; never stir soup with a knife – this last one is very, very bad. Never stir soup with a knife.'

'I never step on a crack. Never,' Emily adds.

'I say chimney, you say smoke, then our wish will not be broke,' Mother Agata adds, singing the words. 'It is impossible to get these things out of one's mind.'

As the room suddenly grows dark, Emily turns and looks out the window and up at the sky. She hears thunder. Enormous drops of rain, the size of a man's fist, fall across the courtyard. Emily turns around and faces Mother Agata. 'Did you ever meet my uncle Charles?' Emily asks.

'No. I never met him. He was already living in Chihuahua. I remember when your parents went to visit him on several occasions. I've only really known your father. Even your mother I only knew for a very brief time since she disappeared soon after I was hired to run the orphanage. Basically, if you think about it, you were raised by me and by your father.'

'Step on a crack breaks your mother's back. Step on a line break your mother's spine. It is incredible how these stupid things stick. Whenever I walk down the pavement I am looking for lines and cracks. I did everything to protect my mother, even this.'

All of a sudden the rain begins to fall with such force against the roof and walls that Emily and Mother Agata can no longer hear each other speak. Thousands of pieces of hail, the size of tiny glass beads, break against the windowpanes.

'I can see the orphans at the zoo,' Mother Agata says as she closes her eyes. 'It's raining very hard. They're all running for cover. They're going to catch cold.'

When Emily gets home from the orphanage she hangs up her raincoat in the hall, places her umbrella by the door and slowly goes up to her bedroom. The house is dark and when she reaches for the light switch beside the stairs she realises that the lights have gone out. In her room she sees that everything looks strange and different, as if a sudden gale had blown through her room and moved everything from its place. The window is wide open. The storm has drenched her windowsill, curtains, and there is a pool of water on the floor with three or four leaves floating in it.

Emily stands in the middle of the room and looks around.

Some of the drawers of her desk are slightly open and her closet door is ajar. Emily notices that a small basket filled with pencils and pens is missing. A photograph of her mother is no longer on her dresser. A group photograph taken of her with the orphans and Mother Agata is gone.

Emily sees that a Chinese jade necklace that hung over the edge of her mirror is also missing.

The tall, three-storey doll's house that stands in one corner of the room and had belonged to Emily's grandmother has also been ransacked. She notices that the small

bed made of mahogany has been taken, as well as the miniature Czechoslovakian crystal chandelier.

She stands at her open closet door and notes that some
of her dresses and blouses hang in disarray. There are also
empty hangers where some of her clothes had been.

Emily feels that everything in her room has been looked
over, touched and examined.

Many of her belongings have been stolen.

Fact:
He raped her because he was drunk.
He raped her because
'She is my wife,' he said.
So Carmela went to her gnawed garden,
with rum-dark saliva
still wet on her cheeks
and cut pods
from the coral bean tree,
broke off spines from the cactus
and picked dry mint leaves.
Again, in the evening,
she made him the tea.
After two spoons of sugar
she spat hard
in the ochre liquid.
All day she makes her sauces and soups,
stirs in pieces of glass

plaster, paint,
her hair, torn shreds
of fingernails
and writes out the recipes
for her daughters.

22.

More 'Terrifying Love'

Emily goes downstairs. Her father is dozing in the living room in front of the lit fireplace. The room smells like burning rosin. A book on insects lies open on his lap. The shimmer from the logs lights up the book's drawing of a pallid yellow praying mantis. The fire also illuminates the silver objects – picture frames, cups and small boxes – that were made long ago from the family's mine. Scattered around the large room, they glow like dozens of mirrors.

Her father wakes up as she walks in. Emily kneels on the floor beside him. He strokes the top of her head. His hand moves down, and down again, over her hair as if his hand were a brush.

Outside they hear the sound of a crier walking down the street. The man calls out in a high-pitched singsong, 'Fix your sewing machine! Fix your sewing machine!'

Emily thinks about the way that Santi sometimes unexpectedly swoops up behind her when she is in the kitchen or looking out of a window. He stands behind her and wraps his arms around her waist and lays his head down on her shoulder. When he does this she hears his breath and smells his skin, a mixture of apples and pencils.

'Father,' Emily asks. 'What did you know about Santi before he came here?'

'Nothing. Really, nothing. I was told about his birth a few years after he was born and so knew that he must be out there somewhere . . .'

'What happened between you and your brother? Why did you lose each other?'

'There's really not much to say. We were always very different,' Emily's father answers as he stands up and places another log on the fire. He stands with his back to the fire. After a short while he says, 'I think he shunned our British heritage and wanted to be Mexican. He hated traditions. I remember that at the age of thirteen he refused to speak in English and would only speak Spanish. I know this disconcerted my parents, but they just went along with him. They went along with anything that he wanted to do. When he left he just disappeared and we lost contact. We were never close. Maybe at one time I thought we were friends in a way, but I was mistaken. I visited him a few times in Chihuahua, after he'd bought that dreadful ranch, but that turned out to have been a mistake.'

'Was the ranch so terrible?' Emily asks.

'Of course I haven't said this to Santi, but it was a god-awful place, in the middle of nowhere with an occasional snake or rabid dog appearing out of nowhere.'

'Did you ever meet his wife, Santi's mother?'

'My brother never even told me he'd married. I actually found out from Mother Agata, who heard it from someone who worked for a church in Chihuahua. Then Santi's mother sent me a letter when my brother died, but that was it.'

'It is strange the way families can just break apart.'

'No, Emily,' her father answers. 'It is not strange. It happens all the time. Sometimes a family can be a dreadful thing. I sometimes think that families could simply be described as unfulfilled expectations. It is not uncommon.'

'Maybe, if he'd lived longer, you might have patched things up . . .'

'A long time ago I learned to eliminate that word "maybe" from my vocabulary.'

'I know, I know, father,' Emily says as she nods her head. 'You hate that word.'

'Yes, there are words one can grow to hate.'

Later, in her room, Emily listens for Santi to come home. An hour later she hears him enter the front door and walk up the stairs. Emily waits for a short while and then goes straight to Santi's room. His door is wide open. He sits beside the sewing machine, holding his accordion between his knees.

'Hello, Santi,' Emily says from the doorway. 'May I come in?'

He looks up and smiles. 'Cousin Emilia,' he says. 'Come in and keep me company. Would you like me to play a song for you?'

'Santi,' Emily says as she walks into his room. She sits on his bed with her arms crossed. 'Were you in my room today? Did you take some of my belongings?'

Santi smiles and places the accordion on the floor beside his chair. He pulls on his fingers so that his knuckles crack. 'Of course,' he answers. 'I was in your room all morning. Nobody was home. I wanted to be with you so, instead, I looked at everything that belongs to you. I took the things I wanted.'

'Please,' Emily says.

'By the way, Emilia (remember I am calling you Emilia now), what are all those newspaper clippings I found? They were all about murders. That was strange . . . and those note-books full of facts. Why?'

'Mother Agata has cut those out for me over the years. It's a joke we have. We discuss them . . .'

'That's odd behaviour for a nun. Don't you think? I have to admit that I decided to leave those behind,' he says and laughs bending his head slightly backwards.

'Please, Santi, can you give me back what you took . . . ?' She opens her hands and stretches them out towards him.

'Those things are mine now,' Santi interrupts. 'They are my spoils. Your father collects butterflies, and I am collecting you.'

'Santi,' Emily says, 'whatever you have taken, I want it all back. I also don't like it that you were in my room looking at everything. It's as though you were a thief.'

'Well, maybe I am a thief. Maybe loving someone is stealing them, in a way. Maybe love is like a slot machine,' Santi says. 'I am not going to give anything back. Everything that is yours is mine. Isn't that what love is supposed to be? Or are you the kind that . . .'

Emily covers her ears with her hands. 'I cannot listen to this,' she says.

Santi looks away from her and begins to sing in a low whisper:

> *When I'm sad she comes to me*
> *With a thousand smiles she gives to me free*
> *It's alright, she says, it's alright*
> *Take anything that you want from me*
> *Anything*

He pretends to play on a guitar. His hair falls over his face. He strums the air. 'Hendrix knew about love,' Santi says.

Emily stands up. She walks over to the sewing machine, touches the hand wheel and spins it around with her finger. This makes the needle go up and down. It is still threaded with the last spool of red thread her mother had placed on it before she disappeared. As a child Emily like to play with the sewing machine, but she never removed the spool of thread.

'You're not serious, are you?' she says. 'You must be joking. I can't believe that you would do this to me.'

'Joking? I have never been more serious in my life,' Santi answers in a controlled, slow voice.

'You're going to keep all those things you took? You don't think you should give them back to me?'

'That's what you heard. That's what I said.'

Santi looks away from Emily and picks up his accordion. It seems to wheeze and cry as he locks it into his hands. He casts his eyes down on the musical instrument and plays a quick scale up and down the buttons.

Without looking at her he asks, 'Did Emily Neale want an ordinary love? Did Emily think we were on a merry-go-round? Did Emily think this was a game? A game of backgammon, poker, bridge?'

'Please! Stop it!' Emily cries as she covers her own mouth with her hand. 'I hate that Inquisition game!'

'Emily, you're not living inside a book any more. You thought the woods were green and the ocean was blue, but they aren't. You were happy in those books, but you're outside now and you are not walking on paper, you're walking in my arms.'

'I liked walking on paper. It held me. I didn't fall. Flowers don't wither in a book. Flowers don't wither in a book,' Emily repeats again. 'By the way, did you read any books? You don't talk about books.'

'No. And I didn't have toys or many friends either since we were so isolated. Inanimate objects were my world; sticks were snakes, the heroic shapes of clouds were gods, and stones had names.'

'My father gave me more dolls and animals than you can imagine. I gave them all to the orphanage. I only really liked books. You can read something that seems strange over and over again until it becomes natural and no longer unusual. You seem so unusual to me . . .'

Santi looks down at his accordion and begins to play a few notes from Astor Piazzolla's *Le Grand Tango*.

'It's getting dark. I can hear the far-off sound of thunder,' Emily says as she stands and walks to the small window in the sewing room that looks into the neighbours' garden. Against one wall is a dark red bougainvillea that looks phosphorescent in the afternoon light. 'A storm is coming. Listen to the birds. Look at the swallows flying towards shelter. I think I'd better go and make sure all the windows are closed.'

'Emily,' Santi says and stops playing. 'Don't you see?'

He grabs Emily's wrist as she tries to walk out the door. He pulls her towards him. 'Don't you see?' he says again. 'I am willing to feed you, iron your clothes, brush your hair and peel your oranges.'

Fact:
She wore a white salwar-kameez. It was the kind that was usually worn by pregnant women.

She placed a sandalwood garland around his neck and said a prayer, 'Lucky are those who are born butterflies.' She knelt at his feet. The Prime Minister stopped to raise her up. She looked at his face, closed her eyes and thought, 'I am a shooting star, a star shooting through the stars.' She closed her eyes and then exploded.

When Dhanu killed Rajiv Gandhi she was wearing a cloth girdle. Stitched into the white cloth were eight bombs packed with eighty grams of C4-RDX explosive and twenty-eight hundred 2 mm steel pellets.

In the hot noon sunlight only six bombs exploded.

Six is the most perfect number. It is both the sum and the product of its parts.

A hexagram consists of two combined triangles, which make six points: the shape of a beehive or snowflake.

Lucky are those who are born butterflies.

23.

And More 'Terrifying Love'

One day Santi decides he is going to fix up the small, abandoned garden so that it will attract butterflies. He says this is a present for Emily's father.

Emily thinks it is just a part of his impulse to control his world. She has watched him leave his shoes and clothes around the house. He has literally taken over every room in the house except her father's bedroom. His books are stacked all over the library and living room. The fruits that he likes and buys, like guavas and pineapples, fill the flat wicker baskets in the kitchen. Emily notices that this behaviour encompasses her as well. He likes to brush her hair, tie her shoelaces and tell her what to wear. Sometimes she thinks he treats her like a child. When she tells him this, he says, 'Yes, you're my little girl.'

Santi spends several days doing research on butterflies from Emily's father's books. He also walks to the plant nursery that is only a few blocks away and buys some sacks of soil, garden tools, and painted ceramic and clay flower-pots. He buys the seeds for ageratum, blue porterweed, butterfly bush, cosmos, hibiscus, and small plants of Mexican flame, heliotrope, dill, fennel, parsley, mustard and wild petunia.

Santi can name the butterflies these plants will attract to the garden. 'Listen to these names,' he says. 'Monarch, queen, large orange sulphur, ruddy daggerwind, great southern white and zebra. Aren't they beautiful?'

'Yes,' Emily answers. 'But you have to realise that I have known and heard about these butterflies for most of my life. My father knows them all so they don't sound very exotic to me.'

Early one morning, when he and Emily lie in her bed in her bedroom, he says, 'You won't believe this, I read that butterflies are territorial and fight, chasing other butterflies out of their territory.'

'They seem so delicate and harmless,' Emily answers.

'Well, it just goes to show there is war in everything and everywhere,' Santi says. He holds the tips of his fingers together in a church-steeple formation.

'What do they fight with? Do they fight with their wings?'

'I will need nectar plants for food and larval plants, which are the food source for caterpillars,' Santi continues without answering Emily's question. 'These plants also provide a place for the butterflies to deposit their eggs.'

'You're really taking this very seriously.'

'I don't do anything half-way,' Santi replies. 'My father used to say that I always lived in a constant state of frustration because nothing is perfect and I want everything to be perfect.'

'My father will be so touched by this,' Emily says. She takes his hand and kisses the inside of his palm. 'Thank you.'

'It is a way for me to do something for him. After all, he let me come here and stay, although I'm a total stranger.'

'Of course he was going to let you stay here. You're family,' Emily says.

Santi holds her close and whispers in her ear, 'You are my kissing cousin. Do you think your father knows?'

'Santi, he suspects nothing. In his eyes I'm still eleven years old. When he sees me he sees braids and ribbons. When he looks into my face he thinks of lullabies. My father still takes my hand to cross the street.'

They remain silent for a while as the room begins to fill with the early morning sun. They are no longer bodies touching and voices in the dark. It is six a.m., and they can now see each other's faces.

'Let me look at your back,' Santi says as he takes hold of Emily's hips and helps her to turn over. He pushes the sheet down to her waist and kneels beside her body. After a few moments, Santi says, 'Yes, I see her.'

'Who? What? What do you see?' Emily asks.

'Do you remember the day we first met, when I was looking at your father's butterfly collection?'

'Yes, of course I remember,' Emily answers.

She lies still as he continues to hold her down with one hand on her back. 'Don't move,' he says as he caresses the length of her back, from her neck down to her tailbone. 'Well,' he continues, 'that evening you told me about Saint Barbara and how architects sometimes see her in bricks and walls and in windowpanes.'

'So?' Emily asks.

'Well, I can see her. She's here. I can see her face in your skin. Your skin is like a marble floor. She's looking at me. She lies inside your bones and holds your heart in her left hand. Now she's closing her eyes. Her mouth is closed and she does not speak. I can see that she is holding a small tower in her right hand.'

Emily does not answer. She lies very still until Santi moves and lies down beside her. She feels cold and pulls the blankets up towards her shoulders.

'It is nice to do something for your father, but mostly I wish he weren't here. If we lived alone together . . .' Santi says.

'What would it be like?' Emily interrupts. 'What do you think it would be like?'

'I know exactly. I've thought about it often. We'd live alone and the house would become a fairytale castle. We'd let cobwebs cover everything. The doors and window frames would become so warped that nobody would be able to open them. You could never leave and no one could ever come inside.'

'Like Sleeping Beauty.'

'Well, what do you think it would be like?' Santi asks as he sucks on her index finger.

'I don't know,' Emily answers. 'Maybe I'd learn to do things I never imagined I could do.'

'What kind of things?' Santi asks.

'Maybe I'd learn how to sing, or knit, or something. Maybe I'd let my hair grow down to my knees.'

'I'd bathe you every morning and every evening.'

Emily smiles.

'I've even thought that maybe we should kill your father,' Santi continues. 'I've had dreams about it. I like to imagine being all alone with you.'

'Santi!' Emily says and covers his mouth with her hand. 'That's not a nice thing to say, or think, or dream.'

'I'm only joking,' Santi says as he kisses the palm of her hand that presses over his mouth.

Emily frowns. 'I know,' she says.

He moves her hand away from his face. Then he takes a long strand of Emily's hair, places it in his mouth and begins to suck on it.

'So,' he asks, 'is there a saint for butterflies?'

'I don't know,' Emily answers. 'I am sure there must be

since there are saints for practically everything. I know that there is one for birds.'

'Tell me about this saint.'

'Saint Gall was an Irish hermit who lived in the seventh century. He was said to have exorcised the daughter of a duke. When the evil spirits left her body they ascended from her mouth as a flock of blackbirds.'

Santi gets up and begins to dress. Emily sits on the edge of the bed and stretches her arms up in the air.

'I used to wonder what it would feel like to have a bird inside my body and inside my mouth,' Emily adds. 'It's strange but, when you're a child, you think of these things.'

Santi stands at the window and looks outside. 'It's drizzling,' he says. 'A dark day.'

'Do you have an umbrella? I can lend you one.'

'I don't mind getting wet, do you?' Santi asks.

'Yes, I mind.'

'You are always protecting yourself, aren't you?'

Emily does not answer. After a few moments she sighs deeply. 'So,' Emily says. 'When are you going to go with me to the orphanage and meet Mother Agata?'

'What did you say?' Santi asks.

'When are you going to go with me to meet Mother Agata?' Emily repeats. 'She keeps asking me about you and I don't know what to tell her any more. I've run out of excuses for you.'

Santi walks over to the side of the bed where Emily is sitting and kneels down in front of her on the floor.

'What did you say?' Santi asks again very slowly, stopping for a long pause between each word.

'Mother Agata,' Emily says. 'When are you going to meet Mother Agata?'

Santi takes both of Emily's wrists in his hands.

'I am never going to meet Mother Agata,' Santi says in a soft whisper that sounds like a low growl. 'Never! Don't you see I hate that nun? She is a pious, good, sweet nun.'

'Santi, please . . .' Emily says as she tries to move away from him. 'What is wrong with you?'

Santi holds her wrists tighter and does not let her move.

'You're all pious. So smug. You and your father disgust me. There is nothing more ugly, more revolting, than the colonial English. Tea on a tray. Sherry. The Queen. Your God damned smug superiority.'

'Please!' Emily cries as she tries to wrestle her wrists out of his hands. 'You're hurting me.'

'How many Mexican men have you screwed? Answer me. Say: not one,' Santi says, holding her wrists with more force.

'Please!' Emily cries again. 'Please, stop. You're hurting me.'

'I'll let go if you say it. Say: not one.'

'Not one,' Emily whispers.

'I can hurt you even more. I can make you cry,' Santi says.

He takes her hand and holds on to her middle finger and begins to pull it unnaturally backwards against the back of her hand, towards her wrist.

'You think you're better than everyone else. So fucking high and mighty, taking care of Mexican orphans . . . Aren't we just so civilised, you think, so awfully good,' he taunts with sarcasm.

'You're going to break it. You're going to break my finger,' Emily says and begins to weep. 'Stop it! Please!'

'Look! You're crying!' Santi says letting go of her finger. 'That's what I wanted.'

'I think you've broken my finger, ' Emily says, looking down at her hand. 'I heard it snap. What's the matter with you, Santi?' she asks as tears begin to flow down her cheeks. 'What do you think you're doing?' Emily pushes him away, but he holds on to her wrists. 'What else are you going to break inside of me?' she asks.

'That's a good way to think about it. I'm breaking you in. I'm making you for me. I learned how to do this on the ranch in Chihuahua, remember? There wasn't a horse I couldn't break.'

He brushes his hands over her cheeks, wetting his hands, and wipes his own face.

'This is what I wanted,' he says, kissing her face. 'I wanted to wash my face with your tears. It's beautiful. I love you.'

Fact:
Nobody can remember her name, although some people recall that she was named after a flower. Her name was Rose, Violet, Lily or Petunia.

Nobody can remember where she came from, although some people recall that she said she was from the North.

Nobody can remember how old she was, although some people think that she was at least thirty-two.

Everybody can remember that she was born in 1895.

Her defence lawyer applied the 'irresistible impulse test' to her case. This test was established in Britain in 1840 and adopted in the United States in 1886. In 1886, the Parsons v. Alabama (81 AL 577, So 854 1886 AL) decision established additional criteria for the insanity defence. The court decided that a person could utilise the insanity defence if he or she could prove that 'by reason of duress of mental disease he had so far lost the power to choose between right and wrong, and to avoid doing the act in question, as that his free agency was at the time destroyed'.

The 'Irresistible Impulse Test' was also known as the 'policeman at the elbow test', a label it had been given by an early court in England. In other words, if the person would have committed the crime even if there was a policeman standing next to him, then the act could be characterised as an irresistible impulse because no sane person would commit a criminal act in the presence of a law enforcement agent.

Everybody remembers that she liked to cut things. She had seven pairs of scissors. She spent hours cutting vegetables and fruits in her kitchen. She cut up books and dresses. She cut her hair.

Some people said that when she ate she cut her raisins, grapes and peas in half. When she sat still she would rub the sides of her hands against her thighs in a sawing motion. She liked to open and close her index and middle fingers, like a pair of scissors, as if she were snipping the air around her.

At dinner parties she liked to pick up her knife and pretend to cut the arm of the man seated next to her.

Everyone said she had irresistible impulses. They said that even if one policeman, or two policemen, or three policemen had been standing right beside her, she could not have stopped herself from killing.

Cut, carve, trim, pare, clip and slice were her favourite words.

24.

When Mother Agata actually says, 'I've Never Lied to You. But I Never Told You the Truth Either.'

It is not the feast day of Saint Francis of Assisi, but this does not matter. Mother Agata thinks that he is such a wonderful saint that she celebrates him at least twice a year. Mother Agata has organised this celebration ever since she began to work at the orphanage and even has a priest come to give a special mass and bless the animals.

The children spend the morning placing chains of flowers around the necks of the three guinea pigs and two white rabbits that are kept in several wire cages on the back patio. The black Labrador gets a wreath of flowers pinned on his head with hairpins. Mother Agata also covers the birdcages in the centre courtyard with garlands. She allows the children to give the animals little pieces of chocolate. It is one of the happiest days at the orphanage.

At noon Emily arrives. 'The Japanese' are on the patio, making chains of daisies. They sit as close as they can get to each other so there is no shadow between them. They tell Emily that Mother Agata is in the kitchen, making lunch.

'She's only making a cake,' Hipolito says as he puts down the flowers and looks up at Emily. 'Because we don't eat meat today.'

'We don't eat the meat of any kind of animal,' Maria adds. 'Not even a chicken.'

'Mother Agata says that we are only going to eat cake today and nothing else,' Hipolito says.

'Yes,' Maria answers. 'It is going to be chocolate cake.'

'That's right,' Emily answers with a smile. She places her hand on Maria's head and tenderly strokes the child's hair. 'One never eats an animal on Saint Francis' saint's day. Do you know why?'

'Of course we know!' Hipolito answers.

The kitchen is a large square room covered with yellow handmade tiles. Clay pots of many sizes are hooked on the wall and braids of garlic cloves tied with red ribbons are draped over the stove. The room smells like fresh cinnamon sticks. Mother Agata is melting a large block of Oaxacan chocolate over the stove. Emily walks in and sits down on one of the bright yellow kitchen chairs that are painted with faded red flowers.

'The cousins said that you'd be here. Of course, I might have guessed,' Emily says.

'I'm glad you're here,' Mother Agata replies as she slowly

stirs the chocolate with a large wooden spoon. 'You haven't been coming as often as you used to.'

'I've been busy with Santiago,' Emily answers. 'He doesn't know the city at all. I've taken him around Mexico and last week I even took him to the pyramids. We stopped to see the Monastery of the Dwarves. That place really surprised him. I think he thought I'd made it up when I first told him about it.'

'So, you've been a tourist guide.'

'Yes, exactly,' Emily answers.

'Does your father like him?'

'Yes, very much. Santi is planting all kinds of flowers in the small back garden to see if they will attract butterflies. He's doing it for my father. Isn't that wonderful?'

Mother Agata takes the pot of chocolate off the stove. Then she takes a large vanilla cake out of the refrigerator and places in on the kitchen table. She sits down beside Emily and begins to coat the cake with the melted chocolate.

'My goodness, what on earth happened to your finger?' Mother Agata asks as she looks at Emily's hand.

'Oh,' Emily says, looking down at her finger, which is wrapped in a gauze bandage. 'I thought it was nothing at first. Now I think that it might be broken.'

'You'd better see a doctor. Is it swollen? It looks as though it might be.' Mother Agata places the spoon in the bowl and takes Emily's hand. She gently touches Emily's finger.

'Yes, it's very swollen and it hurts. I put the bandage on so I won't accidentally bend it. As a reminder more than anything . . .'

'How did you do that?'

'I'm not really sure. It was one of those things. I bent it backwards,' Emily answers and takes her hand away from Mother Agata. 'That cake looks delicious,' Emily adds, dipping her pinkie into the chocolate and tasting it.

'You'd better go and see a doctor,' Mother Agata says.

'Yes, I will, don't worry. Santi thinks I probably just sprained it, but I did hear it crack . . .'

'So, why haven't you brought Santiago to the orphanage?' Mother Agata asks. 'Why hasn't he come here so that I can meet him? Have you told him that his family founded this orphanage? Have you told him that this is one of the city's oldest institutions?'

'I don't know,' Emily answers. 'I don't think he's very religious. I don't think he's very interested in children . . .'

Mother Agata hands Emily the large wooden spoon that is dripping with melted chocolate.

'I suppose you still like to lick the spoon. You always wanted to as a child.'

'Mmnn,' Emily replies, taking the spoon. 'Of course. That's the best part.'

Mother Agata leans back in her chair and sighs. 'This is such a special day,' she says. 'Sometimes I think it is the best holiday of all. I think the animals even know it is their special day. I even imagine them speaking to one another. Isn't that funny?'

'Yes, like something from an animated movie, *Bambi* or something,' Emily says, licking more chocolate from the spoon. 'But maybe they're actually saying that this crazy nun is so confused since it is not our real day at all!'

Mother Agata laughs and adds, 'At least a few days a year we can give animals back their dignity.'

'Yes,' Emily says.

Outside they suddenly hear the loud noise of the apple truck. The truck has a loudspeaker that bellows a recording over and over again: *Lady of the house, lady of the house, come and buy, come and buy, apples, apples, ripe apples, apples that are very cheap.*

'I guess I won't buy any today. I still have some left over from two days ago,' Mother Agata says. 'In any case, that man's apples are not so good. They're too green. He picks them before they're ready.'

'I always buy them at the Coyoacan market,' Emily says.

'Yes, that's where your mother bought them.'

'Yes, I know. She also disappeared from that market. I always think of her when I go there to shop.'

'Emily,' Mother Agata asks, 'I've been wondering, I hope you don't mind if I ask, but why don't you wear your mother's cross any more?'

Emily places the spoon back in the bowl and reaches for her neck, pressing her hand against it. 'I just wanted a change,' Emily says. 'It's nothing, really. Don't worry, I still believe in God.'

After a short pause Mother Agata places the bowl of chocolate to one side. She presses her hands together as if she were praying and asks, 'What's going on, Emily? I've known you for ever.' Mother Agata adds in a soft, kind voice, 'How did this happen?'

Emily covers her mouth with her hand and begins to tremble. 'I don't know,' Emily stammers. 'It was quick. It happened immediately.'

'Well, you know it's foolishness, pure foolishness, so just forget about him.'

Emily feels the smell of chocolate surround her. She feels the sugar from the syrupy icing rush through her body. She rubs her eyes.

Mother Agata takes her hand. A large hand like a large cooking glove. 'There, there,' she says. 'It can't be so bad.'

'He loves me too,' Emily answers, looking away with her eyes cast towards the window. 'He says he will peel my oranges for me. He loves me.'

Mother Agata sits very still. Outside the kitchen they hear the sound of four or five children running down the hallway. They can hear the electric hum of the refrigerator.

After a few moments Emily stands up. 'I think I'll go and help the children decorate the altar,' she says.

'No,' Mother Agata says without letting go of Emily's hand. 'You stay right here and listen to me.'

'There's nothing to say,' Emily answers.

'There's a lot to say. You'd better listen to me.'

Mother Agata stands up. She places her hands on Emily's shoulders and begins to speak.

Emily can smell her breath of oatmeal and raisins.

She can smell her skin, which smells like oatmeal.

Her breath on Emily's face comes in rapid gusts as if she were running. 'Jesus, Holy Mother of God,' Mother Agata whispers after she has finished.

'What?' Emily says as she pushes Mother Agata's hands off her shoulders.

'I've never lied to you. But I never told you the truth either. I made a promise not to tell you. I kept my promise.'

Emily stands up. She walks slowly to the kitchen sink. One, two, three, four, five, six, seven steps. She leans over the kitchen sink and spits. She spits one, two, three times. She thinks about what Mother Agata told her about lying and spitting. Emily wipes her mouth with the back of her hand.

The window over the sink looks down on the inner patio. Emily can see 'The Japanese' sitting as close as they can get to each other so there is no shadow between them. She watches Hipolito lean over and lick Maria's cheek.

'Does Santi know this?' Emily asks as she turns to look at Mother Agata. She suddenly feels as cold as a stone in gravel, as cold as a mossy wall, as cold as a piece of ice. She shivers.

'I don't know. What has he said to you? He may just think he's unlucky.'

'Can love be unlucky?'

Emily walks over to Mother Agata and wraps her arms around her large waist. She presses her head against Mother Agata's chest and can hear her heart. Emily feels like she is embracing the tall wooden mast of a large sailboat.

'You have always been my mother,' Emily whispers. A cloud passes overhead and darkens the room. Emily watches as the shadows lose colour and disappear. 'Please tell me, what does my father know about all of this?'

Mother Agata kisses the top of Emily's head. 'My dear child. He didn't know for years. We thought she really had disappeared and then it hurt too much to change the story. You can't imagine what the man has suffered.'

'Thank you,' Emily whispers. 'Yes, I've watched him suffer every day of my life. We all have. What do I do now?'

'My daughter, His merciful kindness is great.'

'Do you think I'm unlucky?' Emily asks as she stands in the doorway ready to leave.

'Yes,' Mother Agata answers. 'To be honest, yes. You're unlucky, but who isn't?'

Fact:
It is all just bits and pieces, bits and pieces are what I've heard about all my life, just bits and pieces. My mother, she was a domestic in Alabama and just a child when I was born.

I don't know the why of it.

Everybody knew I was crossbreeded. These things weren't explained, they were just there.

It's funny the things you remember in your life. I remember the first time I was allowed to pour the lemonade.

I became a washwoman when I was twenty years old. I learned about all kinds of things working in people's houses like seeing how well people treated their animals and then treated their domestics so poor. Like the dogs and cats got good meat or their food on a china plate and the domestics we got a bologna sandwich on an old chipped plate.

I don't really like to go around telling people my sorrows.

When I left someone's house I always pretended I was coming back when I knew I wasn't. I don't like scenes, or explanations, or people begging you to stay. I'd say see you tomorrow. I'd say see you tomorrow. I said I'll be back tomorrow.

Those people, I hated it, since they always called you by a nickname as if you didn't have your own name, as if they owned you if they named you. Some called me cookie, or ladybird. And I hated it when they gave me cast off, castaway, second-hand stuff. They thought you should feel gratitude. I took that stuff, walked down the street and threw whatever it was into the first garbage can I could find.

I like things to be spick and span, nice and spick and span so washing is not such a bad thing. I also iron. If you wash and iron people's things, well, you really get to know about their lives. Washwomen know all the secrets, I say.

I know how to press all kinds of collars, like a bow collar, sailor collar, bertha collar, cowl neck, stand-up collar and wide and slim lapels. One lady had a blouse with a collaret, which is little ruffles all going round in a circle. It was beautiful and really hard to press.

I had a husband I don't even care to think about. We lived in a little shotgun house. He knew all the ins and outs of me. At first we were easygoing with each other and that man was so pretty. But then he got to thinking I should be at his beck and call. It was just beck and call all day long. And then he'd be real nice. As I said, he knew all the ins and outs of me.

What he didn't know, and it was deep in me and hard to look for, was that one day I would just have had enough, and that would be that. So one day, it was a Tuesday, I remember, I just hit him over the head with a big iron skillet. I never missed him but I threw that skillet away. You can't cook in something that has killed.

You might ask, why a skillet? Well, you use the weapon that you have nearby you. Maybe if the skillet hadn't been near my right hand he'd still be alive today.

I don't even care to think about that.

'Maybe the world is better off without him,' that's what I told myself. I had asked God if I should kill my husband and he said yes. I heard him whisper it. I didn't ask for a second opinion.

The funny thing of it is this. Nobody ever asked anything about anything. I just buried him and that was that. And then I thought about it for some time and I thought, well, for everybody it was just another dead black man who died. So I thought maybe if all

the women killed their black men the whites would be so happy
that instead of jail they'd be giving you a medal. Sometimes it's hard
to think this, maybe it is just a fool thought, and, well, maybe
everyone believed me when I said he sat up and died.

25.

She Walks on Flowers

Emily leaves the orphanage and goes directly to the Coyoacan market; the place where she was told her mother had disappeared. She walks among the stalls of fruits and vegetables, dried chillis, grains and spices. The market smells like the mixed odours of cumin, oregano, roses and chocolate. She can hear an organ grinder play in a distant corner.

Emily stands at the booth that sells pins, needles, spools of thread, crochet pins and knitting needles, and rolls of ribbons and lace. It is the place where no one ever saw her mother. She remembers the police report: *The young girl who sold Mrs Margaret Neale the black thread said she was crying and blowing her nose. When the young girl asked, 'What's the matter?' Mrs Margaret Neale answered, 'I am turning into a piece of silver. The number 925 is branded on my arm. I'm leaving my daughter and I'm leaving my husband because they're better off without me. Nobody will ever forgive a mother who can abandon her child. I am a mermaid like the story of* The Little Mermaid. *My legs are*

*going to turn into a fishtail. I have to go to the sea or I'm going to
die.'*

Emily continues to walk and stops at a stall where, as a
child, she bought miniature buckets, brooms, chairs and a
tea set. She stops at the stall that sells papier-mâché piñatas
of stars and animals.

Outside she wanders through the shops that spill out onto
the street and sell children's costumes. Poised on metal
hangers are the clothes for hiding. There is Little Red Riding
Hood, Minnie Mouse, a fairy, a flamenco dancer, a Hawaiian
dancer, a Mexican revolutionary, Snow White and an Indian.

As a child Emily felt that that the market contained her
mother and that she would reappear one day among the
mangoes, lace and piñatas.

As Emily leaves the market for her house she walks
through the Coyoacan neighbourhood and past the tall stone
walls of the local church that are hundreds of years old. Today
they are covered by graffiti. Someone has painted an enormous blue and green butterfly next to letters that spell out:
MAYBE TODAY. There are also several drawings, captured
roughly in red spray paint, of hands reaching towards the sky.

The last two rains have swept away all the jacaranda and
bougainvillea blossoms from the trees and the water-bruised
flowers cover the pavement. She walks on flowers.

When Emily gets home she sits in the garden for a few
minutes before going inside the house. The garden floor is
covered with stones. There is no grass. It is a garden of

hopscotch and skipping ropes, a garden without butterflies or beetles, and without a swing. One periwinkle blooms in an old clay flowerpot. It is a garden without a brother or sister, a garden without a mother.

Emily walks from the garden into the kitchen. Lying in the sink there is an enormous bouquet of white roses wrapped in white cellophane. She thinks there must be at least four dozen roses in the bunch. The soft smell of the flowers fills the room as she walks towards the hallway and up the stairs.

Emily sits in Santi's room, waiting for him to get back home from work. She sits very still on his bed beside the stained and varnished accordion. She holds the wedding picture of Santi's parents in her hands. Emily looks at the bride's face. Her black hair is braided in a long coil that falls over her left shoulder. Santi's father stands behind her with his hands on her head, as if he were blessing her. She is wearing a simple white dress and holds three white roses in her hand. Her face is unrecognisable since it is darkened and completely erased by Santi's father's shadow. Emily cannot make out the features. In the dark she looks like a piece of obsidian, the beginning of the world, Eve. Emily thinks: it was marriage in a world of rattlesnakes, wolves and mammoth bones.

After half an hour Emily hears the front door open and listens to Santi's footsteps as he walks up the stairs. She places the photograph back on the bedside table.

'Hello, Cousin Emilia,' Santi says as he walks towards her, takes off his jacket and sits beside her. 'My drawings for the church were accepted today. They liked what I did, although they want the ceilings a little higher. But that's no problem. I can fix that up in a flash. God, it's been a long day. I'm so tired.'

'Yes, yes, isn't that good news.'

'What have you been up to?' Santi asks as he slowly rolls up the sleeves of his white cotton shirt.

'Not very much,' Emily answers. 'I was at the orphanage this morning. We had a big celebration.'

'I get my first cheque next week,' he says as he places his arm around her waist, pushes the collar of her blouse to one side and kisses her shoulder. 'When I get the money I will take you out for a wonderful dinner. Would you like that? Where would you like to go?'

'Yes, yes, that will be very nice,' Emily answers.

'Did you get my present? Did you get my roses?'

'Yes, yes.'

'Where are they?'

'They're downstairs in the kitchen. Thank you, Santi.'

'I told the florist to cut the thorns off. I think he thought it was an odd request. I had to repeat myself three times. Cut all the thorns off! I didn't want you to prick your finger. And why do you keep saying "yes"? What is wrong with you? You're acting strange . . . Give me a kiss.'

'I don't think the florist has ever been asked to take off the thorns before . . .'

'I just wanted to protect you.'

'Yes, I see.'

'I didn't know if I should buy you yellow or white. In the end I bought the white roses. Did I pick out the ones you like best? I vaguely remember you telling me that white flowers were your favourite kind.'

'I don't recall saying that. But it doesn't matter. Yes, I love white flowers.'

Emily takes a deep breath and turns towards Santi. She takes his face in her hands and looks into his eyes. She holds her mother's face. She kisses her mother's face. She thinks: *Disappeared. An eleven-letter word. Disappeared like a lost ring, a sweater, and a spoon. Vanished. This is a word with eight letters. Vanished like early morning fog and dew. Vanished into the magician's hat. Lost is a four-letter word. Lost into a genie's lamp. Missing is a seven-letter word.*

In a quiet whisper, in a slow voice, in the voice of a sleep-walker, she tells him everything that Mother Agata told her that morning at the orphanage.

When Emily finishes Santi bows his head and closes his eyes.

'Look at me,' Emily says. 'To think my whole life I've thought something terrible, something really terrible, had happened to my mother when, the fact is, she ran off with my father's brother. It's pitiful. To think how much I worried about her. I was worried that she was hungry or thirsty . . .'

'She was safe,' Santi answers.

'I was her daughter. She knew where to find me.'

Outside they hear the sound of a man's deep voice cry out, 'I will buy your old newspapers, scraps of metal, any junk you have. I will buy your old newspapers, scraps of metal, any junk you have.'

'Did you know this?' Emily asks. 'Tell me you didn't know. Please, tell me you did not know. I feel so cold.'

'Yes,' he says softly.

Emily stands up and moves away from him. 'You make me sick,' she says in a slow whisper. 'Hold your words, Santiago. Don't look at me.'

Santi rises from the bed and begins to walk back and forth in the small sewing room.

'Don't start that!' he says in a deep and angry whisper. 'Don't get so high and mighty. Listen to me . . .'

'You lied. Everyone has lied to me,' Emily answers as she walks over to the closet that is still filled with her mother's clothes. She opens the door and looks in on the rows of clothes hanging on old oak wood hangers. 'She left her daughter as easily as she left her dresses,' she says aloud.

Santi kneels at Emily's feet. He takes her hands in his and holds them tight. He presses his forehead against her leg. 'Forgive me,' he says.

'I didn't fit in the suitcase . . .'

'I never imagined this. I didn't plan it. I promise.'

'Something terrible has happened,' Emily says.

'No,' Santi answers. 'It's not terrible.'

Emily thinks, 'A black bird flew over our heads. We walked under ladders. We stirred the soup with a knife.'

Fact:

It was a joke. It was a game. The first letters of the victims' names spelled MURDER.

They were best friends. They shared their clothes. They liked to comb each other's hair and create fantastic hairdos: large, teased French knots, coiled braids and pigtails. They painted lipstick on each other's mouths.

Gwendolyn Gail Graham was born in 1963. Catherine May Wood was born in 1962. They met while they were both working at a nursing home. They liked to keep souvenirs: handkerchiefs, brooches and sets of dentures, ring and watches.

Forty patients died in the first quarter of 1987. It was a joke. It was a game. They loved to play 'Mother, May I':

Mother, may I dance?
Yes, you may.
Mother may I sing?
Yes, you may.
Mother, may I kill?
Yes, you may.

26.

Dressed in His Clothes

At three in the morning. Emily quietly slips out of her bed
in order not to awaken Santi. The dark morning air feels cold
against her naked body. She tiptoes to the end of the room
and picks up Santi's clothes, which are draped over the chair
of her dressing table. First she puts on his blue linen trousers
and fastens his leather belt around her waist. They hang
loosely on her hips. Then she puts on his white shirt and does
not bother to close up the buttons. She slips her bare feet
into his shoes. She shuffles as she walks so the shoes don't
slip from her feet. Inside his clothes she still feels the warmth
of his body against her arms. His clothes smell like lemons.

Emily moves down the hall past Santi's room and then
along the hall lined with the prints of British castles and past
her father's bedroom. Quietly she goes down the stairs. She
feels her feet inside the cold leather of Santi's shoes and the
shape of his foot under her foot. She walks where he walks.

In the dark kitchen she reaches for a wooden match from

the large box that rests under the windowsill. She pulls back
the sleeves of Santi's shirt and strikes the match and lights the
stove. The room fills with the soft blue light of the gas burners.
She washes her hands in the sink and dries them against Santi's
trousers.

Emily opens a kitchen drawer.

In the drawer there is:

a filleting knife
boning knife
ham knife
carving knife
grapefruit knife
bread knife
cook's knife
oyster knife
and a paring knife.

She takes out the cook's knife and the oyster knife.

Two knives for two hands.

They are not heavy.

Emilia remembers Saint Placid. He is invoked against
chills.

Fact:
*She said that blood on your body was like a warm, new rain – a
morning rain in the rainy season.*

She said that her mother knew that there were some things that were worth killing for and going to jail for, like being lied to or spat on.

She said that blood on your body was like a warm, new rain – a morning rain in the rainy season.

She loved to read books because she said you could kill someone in a book, fall in love in a book, and travel in a book and visit the desert.

She said page 4 can be very quiet.

Page 34 can be the night cry of a watchman.

Page 108 can be a child lost in the forest.

Page 204 can be a night of love and a night of mischief and a night to be eaten by a wolf and a night to wear a glass slipper and and and and and